Charles McLeod's fiction has appeared in publications including *Conjunctions*, *DOSSIER*, *Five Chapters*, the *Gettysburg Review*, the *Iowa Review*, *The Pushcart Prize: Best of the Small Presses*, and on *Salon*. A Hoyns Fellow at the University of Virginia, he has also received fellowships from the Fine Arts Work Center in Provincetown and San Jose State University, where he was a Steinbeck Fellow.

ALSO BY CHARLES McLEOD

American Weather

CHARLES McLEOD

National Treasures

VINTAGE BOOKS
London

Published by Vintage 2013

2 4 6 8 10 9 7 5 3 1

First published in Great Britain in 2013 by Vintage

Vintage
Random House, 20 Vauxhall Bridge Road,
London SW1V 2SA

www.vintage-books.co.uk

Addresses for companies within The Random House Group Limited
can be found at: www.randomhouse.co.uk/offices.htm

The Random House Group Limited Reg. No. 954009

A CIP catalogue record for this book
is available from the British Library

ISBN 9780099542230

Stories in this collection have appeared in the following places, sometimes in
slightly different form: 'Arbor' in the *Gettysburg Review*; 'The State Bird of
Minnesota' in *Michigan Quarterly Review*; 'Edge Boys' in *Conjunctions* and
Pushcart Prize XXXIV: Best of the Small Presses; 'Nycticorax Nycticorax' in
Midwestern Gothic; 'Individualized Altimetry of Stripes' in the *Iowa Review*;
'Rumspringa' in *Five Chapters*; 'Microclimates' in *Post Road*; 'Domestica' in *Alaska
Quarterly Review*; 'How to Steal Electricity' in *Hayden's Ferry Review*; 'National
Treasures' in *DOSSIER* and *Fakes*

'The State Bird of Minnesota' will also appear in the anthology *New Stories from
the Midwest*, forthcoming in early 2013 from Indiana University Press

The █████ ████████ █████ ██████ ███████ ████████ ████ ███████ ████ █████ █████ ████ █████ █████ rdship
Counc███ ███ ████ ███ ████ ████ ███████ ████ ████ ████████ ███████ ████ ███████████ nisation.
Our ███ ████ ███ ████ ████ ███ █████ ████████ █████ ████ █████ █████ █████ l paper.
FS ████ ███ ████ ████ ████ ████ █████ ████ ███ █████ ████ ███ ████ ████ ████ ading

Typeset i█ ████ ████████ █████ ████ ████ ████ ████ ██████ Stirlingshire
███████ ████ ████ ████ ████ ████ ████ LC

ARBOR

She's not thinking about trees yet, but she's going to. It's autumn; the leaves have started to turn. On her way out the door, it's car keys and pigtails, the music in her head turned up. She's had her license since April. The summer was wondrous. The Cape filled with people. The beaches, the boys. But more than the boys, the worth that driving afforded her, the growth, the long hours of sun and salt air and gulls' calls, the windows half-mast in her old-model Prelude, the Cape bathing, the Cape bathed, every small limb of road discovered, the disease of begging rides from her parents shrugged off, beaten with the blink of the camera's shutter in the Brewster DMV. Here were the white dunes north of Truro. Here were Chatham's jetties, the worn planks of docks, the El Toros tied and bobbing. Her best friend – who could not yet drive, and would later become an alcoholic and move far away, to Oregon, and not visit her in the hospital, even after letters were sent, even after her own parents had sent the friend letters and had contacted the friend's parents around Christmas time, when they imagined that the friend would return home regardless of personal success or failure, because that is what children did at Christmas time, they

3

returned home – unbelted and chain-smoking, punching at the radio's buttons: seek, seek, seek, seek, seek. When she remembers the summer, she remembers in fragments. The verse of a song. The fin of a humpback. The dull click of the car lighter, its knob popping out, the coils of heated metal glowing orange.

She is running late. She is always running late. She is holding a cup of coffee and has just jumped the set of five wooden stairs that separates the porch from the concrete walkway. Behind her, her mother is saying something. She feels the coffee slosh inside the slim metal cup, the contents hitting the plastic cap, a trickle of liquid escaping through the mouthpiece. She jumps and lands and the shock absorbs through her black canvas sneakers, through the soles of her feet. It is early October. It is 7:23 in the morning. The air in Orleans is sewn tight with mist. She is on her way to Hyannis, to take her PSATs. What is her mother saying? She is repeating a word. She loves her mother except that she speaks incessantly. Her father worked bonds but had a heart attack and retired. Now he paints canvases of the sea. In the back of his Saab is a folded-down easel. Whole days are spent at the lot at Nauset, between the lighthouse and the long flight of steps that lead to the beach. Their house has three bedrooms, but she doesn't have siblings. She's put together slowly, unintentionally – the way a moon is pulled into the orbit of a planet – that there was supposed to be a brother or sister and that some event stopped this from happening. All thought on the subject ends here, however, via the mental image of her parents, horizontal. Even though she is unmitigatedly interested in this act herself. Even though the Prelude has seen its fair share of fumblings, the boys at her ink-colored J. Crew underwire bras like raiders at an archeological site, trampling the treasures they hope to possess and in their small, crude ways influencing history.

Now she is past the fence's low wooden gate, its coat of white paint pristine. The key hits the car's lock and the lock's tumbler turns and with a single finger she pulls up the door's plastic handle. Over summer she has mastered these angles and motions, has learned the ballet of entry. Her knees bend, her hips pivot, her posterior lands square on the cold, faux-leather seat. Again the coffee sloshes, the sound tidal, a lapping. The engine turns over and the dash meters light up. For the last time she reverses out of the driveway. She will come to hate cars, when she can no longer walk, when entering a vehicle involves the assistance of poorly paid orderlies, strong men with grim pasts who grew up without dreams, whose social and fiscal avenues of possibility did not often transcend the learning of how to curl one's fingers into the trademarked symbology of certain murderous fraternal orders, of gangs, those consortia relegated, by myriad factors, to short lives of violent gluttony. In the years ahead it is these men who will touch her most, a forearm slid beneath her wrecked legs, passed under her at the back of the knees, and she will raise her arms and one of these ex-offenders, these minimum-wage parolees, will bend to meet them, lifting her from prison to prison, from belted seat to belted seat. There will be bedsores and catheters, a cadre of nurse aids. There will be a physical therapist who leads her through physical therapy, which does nothing, the motor neurons useless with no synaptic bridge, her muscles forever atrophied. There will be long nights with no sleep, and by chance her room will be a corner room, and what do the windows of this room look out on? They look out on trees. Specifically the great maples of historic New England, their autumn colors a consistent source of nostalgia and bad poetry, both of which the girl will possess in abundance, as she lies in her gurney with pad and blue ballpoint, putting adjectives to memories of her terminated bipedalism, of standing, without aid, on her feet.

The word that the mother keeps saying is *carefully*. The mother chooses the adverbial form of the word in an attempt to sound other than worried. The mother watches the daughter jump because this is what a mother does: watches her child – what she brought into the world – jump, jump repeatedly. Jump from chairs, jump from stools, jump from the lip of a pool and sink beneath. Jump from the back of a brown leather sofa. Jump from any number of places the child was never supposed to be. Jump into grade school. Jump into puberty. Jump from literal to figurative jumping, the ledges growing higher and at the same time more abstract. The child jumps and there is the mother's heart, jumping.

In the square, fenced yard, the lawn dewed and mowed and green, her daughter is caught again in mid-air. At college the child will flunk out, win awards, spend long Sundays imbued with golden light from the high windows of a library. The child's future is a bed of seeds that sprout nightly in the brain of the mother, as she turns beneath then readjusts the bed sheets. So the word the mother chooses, must always choose, is *carefully*, because the mother must say it a thousand times – more – and hope that just once it will hold in her daughter's brain, because the mother's own parents are now long dead, buried in this country's rusting breadbasket, and specifically on the outskirts of Wausau, Wisconsin, where the mother herself spent all of her youth before her own migration, her own jumping, and her husband, whom she loves, is not all that well, and both his parents, her in-laws, are dying, and in recent months, she, the mother, has started more fully to comprehend and accept a great, grand conclusion to everything, and that because each thing's conclusion is so great and so grand, and because death weathers life so effortlessly, the mother, even now, as her daughter speeds off, must say the word again, whisper it to herself, and hope that the fog can act as conductor.

Her head is pressed to the roof of the car; the Prelude has flipped itself over. She is upside down on Highway 6. She is moving at a high rate of speed and is about to pass off the shoulder. The cap has come off the top of her coffee. The liquid goes everywhere, soaks in, is gone. This concerns her, though it won't very shortly. What was she doing to arrive here, to this? There was a song on the radio; she'd meant to be studying. There were cue cards with word pairs in a pile on her dashboard. Her cell phone was ringing, is ringing now, as she glides toward disaster. Out of the corner of her eye, in her vision's periphery, the cell phone is blinking and chirping, and this digital ephemeron had been seconds earlier of utmost importance, because the number displayed on the cell phone's bright face was unequivocal, was none other, was the number of the boy that she'd thought of all summer, who should have but never once called her, whom she gazed at from the far sides of bonfires and parking lots as he wandered with and shoved at his pack of problemed followers: fat boys, meek boys, boys steeped in drugs, boys with hate in the pits of their hearts, boys with no real futures, and he led them, this boy, the one that she wanted, led them to food, led them to liquor, led them over the last dune on the beach and into the thick of the party. *He* was calling her. He was a senior. He had a black leather jacket he'd bought in Manhattan. He'd gone there to visit his sister. He'd walked through Chelsea, had a lunch of Cuban food, specifically a pulled-pork sandwich, and went with his sister, a junior at Tisch, to a boutique, and purchased the jacket. He'd used the credit card lent to him by his father, the ebony Amex, given over reluctantly from the father's leather wallet and with the stipulation it be used only in case of emergency, that it be placed in the boy's Velcro wallet and drawn out only should something unforeseeable happen, which it had, that event being the seeing of the jacket, certainly something the boy had not planned to lay eyes on, and which therefore, under the strict definition of the word, existed in the realm of the 'unforeseeable' and thus justified the drawing-out of the Amex and handing it over to the boutique's clerk, the card's plastic the same rich black as that of the jacket.

He'd told her all this at a party on the beach, very early in the springtime. There was frost on the dunes, a gibbous moon overhead. Both of them were drinking from red plastic cups filled with fruit juice and purloined liquor. In the bonfire light his cheeks had seemed bronze. She was freezing and barefoot and tipsy. Her friend had gone farther down the beach's long shore with the football team's starting tail-back. There were waves and din, then the verse of a song – someone had remembered a boombox, and with the flip of a switch a frenzy ensued, the attendees' yawping Dionysian, for the song that came on was one of those songs, overproduced and sentimental and fleeting, a song designed to move units and vanish, but in its short life so very important to this country's army of teenagers, its enlisted driven by ego and the need to belong, or have people in positions of influence and power – specifically quartets of white twenty-something males – affirm that it was okay not to belong, that no one belonged, and that through this disunity all were united. A rock ballad, that standard-issue artillery of Top 40 radio, had filled up the night-time. The partygoers brayed in recognition, and this had made the boy smile and she had smiled back and they had talked more and then been re-absorbed by the party, gone their separate ways without a real goodbye, and she thinks about this as the car leaves the asphalt for the sand-marled pitch, the Prelude totaled, turning over and over, and it is after one of these flips that her temple connects with the car's metal frame, knocking her out cold, unconscious, a loss she remembers as reaching the center of a smooth, white stone, as crossing the threshold of somewhere she had never thought to enter.

The tree the car hits is a *Pinus rigida*, a Pitch Pine, that most stalwart and homely of conifers. It is the Pitch Pine that can endure the salt air of the Cape; it is the Pitch Pine that constitutes most of New Jersey's famed Barrens. It is the Pitch Pine that takes its name from its high resin content, giving the evergreen a storied resistance to decay, and for this it was the Pitch Pine, at one time, that was chosen for a variety of human endeavors: the building of ships, the reinforcement of mine shafts, the making of ties for the railroads of the Northeastern Corridor. From the Pitch Pine white settlers fashioned beams and baulks and joists, manufactured turpentine and rosin, and it was the pulp of the Pitch Pine, refined to paper, on which de Tocqueville wrote down what he saw during his tours of the American process, when it was decided by the Frenchman that the cornerstone of a young democracy was to be *a shared, written language*, that progress was most heavily reliant upon communication, and that if one could not communicate one would not proceed, which meant nothing good for the Indians, though from the beginning this idea seemed non-negotiable. So the knots of the Pitch Pine were put to work, ignited, held as torches by the burgeoning Anglo, the meat of the tree turned to fodder and metaphor, fixture and symbol, for it was the Pitch Pine that, torn down, could be given shape; it was the Pitch Pine, dismantled, that stood for something. And the Pitch Pine, resilient, grew and regrew, had outsmarted hazards millennia prior, when the gravest threat faced by any species of flora was not the acts or the awls of industrious men but that of fire, of elemental consumption, to which the Pitch Pine adapted by sprouting new branches from its bole, producing sub-trunks, so that the Pitch Pine, hydra-headed, might lose part of itself but not all of itself, might have limbs mutilated beyond hope of repair and still, in some manner, function.

The care ward lies on ten acres of land on the limits of Concord, New Hampshire. The building is brick, four stories, L-shaped. Its full name is New Vistas Recovery Center. In the girl's three years of residence one person has recovered, a middle-aged truck driver with the full name of Vance Earl Tackett. Vance Tackett hauled timber and shot crank on the clock. Vance Tackett was a fan of 'new country'. Vance Tackett had a wife taking him to Family Court *fucking always* because Vance Tackett was the father of two, a boy and a girl, but didn't think they needed his money. In Vermont, October, 1999, at 9:18 in the evening, Vance was in third gear and heading south toward the city of Boston. A turn in the road had presented itself abruptly, and Vance Earl Tackett had failed to downshift. His trailer, a double-axle flatbed stacked heavy with lumber, had pulled him off the blacktop and into the forest. The cab turned; the cab fell. Vance Tackett was not wearing his seat belt. Vance Tackett had not slept for seventy-two hours, could not have slept if he had wanted to, so altered was the chemistry of his bloodstream. The truck left the road and at impact Vance Tackett experienced his lumbar incident, the injury given cadence via two small pops in his spine's lower region, twin noises which Vance did not hear but could feel, his legs turned to dead weight, inutile. After an airlift, an ambulance and five hours of surgery (and the surgeon was good, bright, young and motivated, sure of himself, as a surgeon must be), Vance Tackett woke up and was declared a cripple. The surgeon, of course, did not use this word, would not even after Vance used it, asking the question *So am I a cripple?*, to which the surgeon replied, looking Vance straight in the eyes, *You will spend the rest of your life in a wheelchair.*

And for five years Vance Tackett did just this, chain-smoking menthols in a corner of the rec room, the paraplegics of New Vistas involved in tournaments of ping-pong while the quads kept score, mute with envy. Here was the heiress, T-boned while driving; here was the Marine from Southie;

here was the criminal shot by his victim; here was the
teenager who had totaled her Honda. New Vistas could
accommodate two hundred in total, and Vance Tackett hated
all of them equally, his nicknames and phrases for his
brethren vitriolic, the meek of the ward doing all in their
power to avoid him, while the resigned, that minority that
had accepted its fate and embraced it, worked hard to sway
Vance whenever they could, to talk with and laugh at and
include him in things, so that one day Vance Tackett too
might be blessed and continue to grow as a person. Which
Vance mocked. Which Vance called *bullshit*. Which led sometimes to fist fights between Vance and the Marine from
Southie, the two men transformed to depraved modern
jousters, rolling at each other over the ward's checkered
linoleum. And like many of New Vistas' other admittances
Vance Earl Tackett had money, settlement checks afforded
him by the Local 482's, his truck drivers' union, their bevy
of lawyers suing the county then the state for the road's
lack of guard rails. The checks arrived monthly, a portion
garnered for past non-support, and much of the rest Vance
spent betting on baseball, which was what he was doing one
night after dinner, had four hundred dollars of his personal-
injury money in a cookie tin on a low table in front of him,
his Blue Jays down 5-3 to the Orioles in the ninth and final
inning. But then a pinch hitter; men were on base. Vance
Earl Tackett was hitting the arms of his wheelchair. The
cookie tin (once filled with buttered Danish shortbreads)

held bills of every denomination, and should this major-league athlete hit the ball from the park the pot would be Vance's, the other men of the ward all choosing the underdog, their dislike of Tackett so very strong that they'd rather lose outright than share in his winnings.

And what did the man do, the bulky Dominican, his lifeblood the American pastime? He took a ball, then a strike and then stepped from the batter's box, knocking the dirt of the infield from his cleats. He stood there. Tackett was still banging, his brown beard unkempt, his thin legs kept warm by a blanket. On his black T-shirt were soup stains and a silk-screen print of the singer Alan Jackson. The pinch hitter stepped in and there was the pitch, a poorly thrown slider left to hang in the air like a wind-taken kite, and then the pinch hitter connected. And as the ball climbed a sound came from Tackett, a deep, low, animal rumble, a noise whose timbre was so bass at first that it verged on being imperceptible, but as the ball lifted so did the sound's pitch, and when the ball left the field for the cheap seats at Camden, Tackett's joy became boundless, his triumphant whine ascending through each octave until Tackett, possessed, pushed up from and out of his wheelchair.

He fell immediately, but it was how he fell, his back hitting the corner of the low table housing the cookie tin, and no one paid much notice at first – Tackett was not liked, and had taken their money. But as Tackett lay there, moving one leg then both (the movements were of the smallest of increments), an understanding crept into the ward's other residents: something inside Tackett had fixed itself. Orderlies were screamed for; the heiress was crying, as was the Marine from Southie. Tackett lay supine, his knees turned to the side, the blanket tucked up to his hip bone. And it was true what they saw, had witnessed a miracle, or at the very least a medical anomaly, for Tackett, wide-eyed and there on the floor, was now moving his ankle ever so slightly. And the miracle progressed, Tackett in tears, pulled back into his chair by the orderlies, and doctors were called and these doctors ran tests, and what they found was that Vance Tackett would indeed walk again, that the angle at which Tackett's back hit the table had caused a decompression of the nerve roots in the *cauda equina*, so that in weeks Vance was dragging himself down the ward's corridors with the help of a walker and nurse's aide, and during the first week of 2006, Vance Tackett, hunched over dual steel canes, managed out of the brick ward forever.

The girl remained there. Around three sides of New Vistas are flat lawns of kempt grass, over which run smooth wide asphalt pathways, and when the weather is mild or merciful in character, some of the patients take to these avenues. She is among them, and likes autumn best, the maple leaves dying on their branches, the grounds of New Vistas not unlike the groomed quads of one of the colleges she never attended. Benches are set alongside the tarred routes, so visitors may sit with the residents. Her mother comes here the first Sunday of each month; she brings picnic food in a wicker basket, an item the girl remembers from youth, can recall picking up and running off with. Her father has worsened; there was a stroke, and now small things – the reading of words, the filling of cups – have become unfeasible. And when the mother talks of planning trips to the Oregon coast or to Wisconsin, to see the graves of her parents, the girl wants to say *You don't understand, every minute is pain, every movement*, but these thoughts are never given a voice; after all, it is her mother. And she does have her poems to keep herself occupied, takes her notebook and pen with her always, and in one corner of the grounds, set back from the pathways, is an ancient and weathered edifice, its wood latticework streaked with peeling white paint – at one point someone had applied a coat of primer, but this task, once completed, was never added to, no further color was implemented, and for this she feels kinship with the leaning, overgrown wooden structure: like her, it is a project unfinished. The great maples stand tall just yards away; there is a deer path that snakes back into the forest, and she has thought often about seeing how deep she could manage to go back into the trees, how she might be surrounded by but also not touching them, and in this manner repair their first major meeting, when things had turned out so terribly, but by the time she has pushed herself across the mowed swatch of lawn (her arms, those limbs, are stronger than she ever thought possible), she is happy enough to wrest her body from its chair and sit very still with her paper and ballpoint, on the carved wooden bench of the arbor.

THE STATE BIRD
OF MINNESOTA

Ludd lived way out on the north side of the lake. No one really ever went over there. His cabin was built up right to his dock, and in the summer Ludd would often go swimming. He was bearded and awkward, an oaf of a man, but in the water he was something to look at. Ludd could hold his breath longer than anyone I've known. You could watch him dive in, go take your meds, and when you came back Ludd would still be down there.

His dock's pilings were dressed with what he'd found while submerged: fishing lures, the handlebars from a children's bicycle. There too was a raft Ludd had fashioned from logs and the tanned hides of animals – badger and deer and foxes. Late afternoons, as the light bowed and stretched, Ludd would untie and drift until sunset. He lay perfectly still, his arms at his sides, legs brought tightly together, and when the light hit the lake at just the right angle, and turned the water golden and orange, Ludd and his vessel looked set ablaze, his raft transformed to a pyre.

Winter our cabins were the only ones inhabited. The white-outs were constant, the lake like a field. On warm days the temperature reached up to zero. Icicles as long as stalactites hung from the rain gutters. A service road was cleared each month by a bulldozer, though neither of us had any use for it. By Thanksgiving I'd taken out the battery from my pickup. Ludd didn't even have a driver's license.

I considered those months, and still do to this day, as a time of very deep privacy. The smallest of things – a goshawk overhead, the tracks of a wolverine left on a snow bank – would linger and echo in the halls of my mind well into the reaches of evening. Halloween weekend, my only autumn there, a blizzard had started near lunchtime. I was excited for the silence the snowfall would bring; I was trying to get to know myself better. Near dusk I heard noises past the living room's window. With two fingers I parted the slats of the blinds and saw Ludd kneeling by the side of my cabin. Some minutes later he thumped up the steps in moccasins he had handcrafted. I opened the door and gave him a nod. Ludd nodded back at me. In his hand was my garden hose. Ludd had coiled it.

'Cold gets up through the spout,' Ludd said. 'Burst all your pipes open.'

I was embarrassed and took the hose from him.

'Don't hear this poorly but once the snows come, I like things to be kind of quiet. Flooding means maintenance and maintenance means people. And I'm not a people sort of person.'

He was so much to look at I forgot to speak. Ludd was six-eight or six-nine, and must have weighed close to three hundred. His beard was jet black and ran the length of his neck. His long nose looked sharp at the tip of it. Ludd's eyes sat so wide apart from each other that his lashes almost met with his sideburns. But what I mean to say is when Ludd's gaze met your own, it seemed he was looking around you, that something urgent stood always in his vision's middle distance, constantly demanding his attention.

'I put rags in your faucets. Keep 'em covered till spring.'

'Okay,' I told him.

'Good enough?' Ludd concluded.

'Good enough,' I said back.

Ludd nodded his head and walked down the steps. I saw him again seven months later.

In St Paul I'd been married and held a nine-to-five job. I worked for a firm that managed wholesale securities. I was expected to take clients' money and invest it somewhere so that it could make more money, which would in turn be reinvested, so the process could repeat. The first symptoms of breakdown occurred at the four-year mark. In my truck, in the company parking garage, I wept often and for no real reason. At night at the dinner table, across from Michelle, I would forget that I was supposed to be eating.

'What's wrong?' she would ask.

'Nothing,' I would say. But what I was thinking was, *Something's coming. I don't know what it is, but there's something on the way. And you and I are powerless to stop it.*

I slept less by the week, and then not at all. In the blue light of predawn, waiting out the alarm, I began to grow paranoid. In a closet or crawl space or down in our basement, someone was waiting. Most often these men had tools of some sort, carpenters' drills or pairs of thin-nosed pliers with which they meant to enter into my brain, and redirect its circuits and pathways. Still later I believed they already had, and that they were following me to check on my progress.

'Are you seeing anything? When you close your eyes?' All the nurses' scrubs were the color of lilacs.

'Sometimes I see birds, eagles or geese. They're flying north, but their wings are on backwards.'

In the psych ward different doctors asked questions from a list. Is there unresolved grief? Are you addicted to drugs? Have you recently experienced the death of a loved one? But it was none of these things, and the inquiries dwindled, and after a month the chief resident halved my dosage. Six weeks later I signed off on my release.

I was sick, and then I got better.

The one modern amenity I knew Ludd possessed was a battery-powered amateur radio. All summer long, from

Ludd's side of the lake, came a tinny extravagant music, accompanied by the extremely high voice of a female. At first I thought the language in which the woman sung to be Mandarin or Korean. Later, I decided it was Hindi. Ludd kept the volume up so he could listen while adrift, and, when the wind blew from the north, the sound would carry all the way to my cabin.

The western edge of Minnesota holds grasses common to the prairie: bluestem and dropseed and miscanthus. Much of the rest – the Central Lakes, the Arrowhead – is coniferous forest. There is also, however, a thin band of deciduous flora: swamp ash and bronze birch and poplars. The lake sat in the northern pocket of this biome; we were closer to Manitoba than Minneapolis, right on the borderland's border.

Ten cabins in total circled the shore. The land was state land, and the dwellings still stood due to a grandfather clause – they had been there before anyone decided the area needed protecting. This clause also meant no renovations could be made; there was no flipping of property. The structures would remain in their original form until time or climate destroyed them.

The last week of May, Ludd took to the lake. Patches of ice still clung to the shore; I stood watching from the porch of my cabin. Ludd was bare-chested and wearing camouflage shorts. The length of his beard and chest hair was uniform. He gave me a wave and then ran the dock's planks in a loping, staggered sort of gallop. It was like watching a sack filled with marbles roll down a hill. Ludd crashed into the water then emerged supine, swimming in a perfect backstroke.

Later that morning the music came on. I decided to go ask Ludd about it. The summer crowd would not show until later, in June, and none of them ever really stayed long. Nearly all came with children and, aside from the lake, the area held no attractions. Most made the trip because their parents had done so, as their parents had before them. The properties were less places of escape than heirlooms they'd been forced to inherit.

Ludd's cabin was an A-frame of unpainted cedar. Humps of snow bunched at the base of the roof, inches from the tarpaper shingles. An overturned wheelbarrow, its belly rusted through, lay next to a washbasin wrapped in sheet plastic. Behind the structure stood a wide grove of bur oaks, the forest continuing north all the way into Canada. Around the oaks' trunks different items had been tied: old license plates, the belt chain from off of a hot saw. The front door opened onto Ludd's dock; there was no way to reach it from the lake shore. I turned the cabin's back corner to find a window to knock on and ran chest first into the barrel of Ludd's rifle.

'Heard you coming,' Ludd said. The gun's action was bolted.

My time in an office had trained me to always be wrong.

'I'm sorry,' I said. I put my hands in my pockets so Ludd wouldn't notice them shaking.

'I've got an errand to see to. Is there something you need?'

'I came over to ask about your music.'

Ludd swung the gun's barrel onto his shoulder. 'It's bothered you,' he said.

'It hasn't,' I said. 'I just want to know what language it's sung in.'

Ludd looked at me with his strange, distanced eyes. He was dressed in all black: tight-fitting pants and big loggers' boots and a thick, ribbed ebony sweater. 'It's Tagalog,' Ludd told me. 'Filipino. Comes in daily from outside of Quezon. I pick it up low-band on my Ten-Tec.'

'All right,' I said, and started walking away. I felt stupid for being so eager.

'A person who turns on a gun is dumb, crazy or brave,' said Ludd. 'And you're not the first or the last of them.'

I stopped walking and spun on my heel. Ludd was smiling at me. His teeth were a mess, not aware of each other; they sprung from his gums at all angles.

'Where's your wife?' Ludd asked. 'You got on a ring.' He pointed the gun's barrel at one of my pants' pockets.

'She's in the Twin Cities. But she's not my wife anymore. Or she is, I guess, for a little while longer.'

Ludd looked toward my cabin, then north to the woods.

Two hours southwest, in the town of Roseau, my divorce papers waited in a PO Box.

'You been out to the shrub-carr? I'm headed that way.'

I shook my head no; aside from day hikes down a deer path I'd found, I'd spent much of the wintertime reading.

'You're welcome to come but we got a long walk.'

'I don't want to intrude.'

'You already did that,' Ludd told me.

From the lake we wound east through high manna grass and a shrub layer of alder and dogwood. New buds dotted the trees' narrow boughs. Red mottled soil sucked at our boot soles. Wild mint grew next to grape fern and patches of bugleweed. We walked single file, everything still, only the two of us moving. The late-morning light turned the air a bright gray. Our plumes of breath curled, then vanished.

A compass was built into the stock of Ludd's rifle, though he never once took a look at it. He'd lived wild long enough that the landscape meant more. The wetlands were his grocery, his drugstore, his strip mall. Over the course of my time – one year – at the lake, Ludd would on occasion impart pieces of knowledge. I learned seeing geese before May meant a drought year was coming. I learned the berries from a winterholly bush could cure fever. But to me Ludd's facts were only that – facts, data that were interesting but useless.

The things that he knew how to put into use I could never have implemented.

After an hour of walking the wood opened on to a meadow. Thin turns of water striped the low field. The clearing stretched out ahead of us for two or three acres. The fog had burned off and the warm sun felt good. Ludd let me catch up and then raised his arm, pointing with a finger.

'Across there,' Ludd said. 'See where the high willow starts? Animals want to be on the edges.'

'Where did you learn how to use a ham radio?' My grandfather had once owned a Ten-Tec.

'Air Force,' Ludd said. 'I was stationed at Clark down on Luzon till '90.'

'You used to fly planes?'

'No, I fixed air conditioners. Other stuff, too. Patched circuit boards and built fuse boxes. But mainly it was A/C units. It was hot down there.'

'They taught you all that while you were enlisted?' I asked.

'Learned it before I went in,' Ludd told me.

'Where?'

Ludd slung his rifle from off of his shoulder and knelt on one knee. 'Princeton,' he said, and then fired.

I wasn't prepared for the report of the gun. The sound stunned me, and for a moment I panicked. In an arc, like a wave, my old life rose up and washed over me. Here was the nurse, her long-needled syringe. Here were the imagined footsteps of men, moving quickly up our staircase in the night-time. My back tensed and I shuddered. I couldn't catch my breath. I'd shut my eyes without realizing I'd done so. When I opened them again, Ludd was headed for the high grass on the far side of the clearing.

What Ludd had shot was a moose, a fully grown bull. It lay dead on the ground, its head peeking out past the stalks of the willows. Its long body was gaunt. Mange patched its fur. Ludd had put a bullet through one of its eyeballs.

'They drop their antlers in autumn, after they mate. Conserves energy for winter.'

Ludd kicked the beast and for a moment it twitched. I looked at the animal's lean, umber muzzle. There was a patch of bare skin just under its nose that was freckled with blood spatter. I hadn't seen the creature at all, and didn't know how Ludd had.

'What are you going to do with it?' I asked.

Ludd shook his head. 'Can't get it back. Weighs half a ton. Stay here a second. I'm going to go check on something.' Ludd handed me his gun and walked back through the willows. I was still breathing hard, my heart high in my chest. It seemed to me against Ludd's ways to kill something and leave it. I didn't understand, and wouldn't for years, why he had shot it in the first place.

From behind me, back on the fringe of the wood, came

a shrill eerie clucking, followed by a rapid series of honks. I turned in time to see a pair of large black and white birds, loons, leaving their hiding spot in the shrub brush. They flew out over the meadow and then circled back in the lake's direction. They had yet to drop their coarse winter coats and their undersides were the purest of whites, and I tried to imagine what must be at work for nature to change the very color of something, to better ensure its survival.

When Ludd came out from the willows his pants were two-toned, wet all the way to mid-thigh.

'Did you see them?' he asked. He was grinning again.

'The loons,' I said.

'The state bird of Minnesota,' Ludd answered.

In remembering my marriage one sequence of images returns to me over and over. These depict man's early attempts at machines meant for flight. One sees these contraptions on commercials, sometimes; they are used popularly as symbols of failure. The film reels, grainy and sepia-toned, show a pair of people in the cockpit of some laughably faulty apparatus. There is the plane with the too-long, tri-tiered wings; there is the plane with the giant umbrella, its pumping locomotion believed by its makers to be enough to lift their craft skyward.

Where I live now, on the Gulf Coast, I encounter sometimes the sort of couple I'd once been a part of.

They are costly and loud and see the Earth as little more than something to keep well below them. In the bayou's June heat they wear black linen suits and hatch plans to develop the flood plain. Their shoes are sharp-tipped and look sleek as jets. Cell phones sit on their hips like missiles.

Soon after my return from the ward, Michelle decided our days together were numbered. She was a lawyer and while there was love, there was also a blueprint that had not been followed correctly. Weakness of character equated to a flaw in design. Our machine would not leave its runway. The securities firm, unsure of how to proceed, let me go with a check in the low sixes. My third Monday home Michelle returned late from work with a brief that she had drafted. This document outlined, in tedious detail, the reasons for our impending separation. There were pie charts and bar graphs that showed, in full color, my drag on our upward mobility. Our living room a court, my wife made her case, pacing the carpet like she was waiting for take-off.

'In the term power couple which word comes first?' she asked me.

I couldn't argue. But I also didn't care. On the coffee table in front of me, I'd opened the paper to the classifieds. In black block letters was the ad for the cabin. **ESCAPE TO THE NORTH**, read the posting.

Everyone's an inventor, whether they know it or not;

survival, alone, is inventing, and our days and our weeks are like wire and bearings, and with each year we add to our chassis. We may not know why we're building but we build anyway. And on occasion, the things we are able to create force others to stop and take notice.

One of Ludd's bombs blew the arm off a child, a sixth-grader named Tiffany Stevenson. Tiffany lived in a suburb of Denver. Her father, R&D for Lockheed Martin, was the package's intended recipient. Wrapped in brown butcher paper, the address in black ink, the square parcel was delivered to the Stevensons' doorstep. Alone in the house and on Christmas vacation, Tiffany could think only of presents. She brought the package inside, taking scissors from their place in a cupboard. With the twine cut the bomb shifted and set itself off. Neighbors called the police. Paramedics were able to save her.

A second device was sent east to New Gloucester, Maine, home to the last surviving community of Shakers. In journals found later, in the cabin at the lake, it was explained by Ludd that his reason for targeting this group was to bring about the Shakers' resurgence; Mother Ann Lee, the sect's figurehead and matriarch, had predicted a revival in Shaker theology once only five members remained in the congregation. This prophecy has so far turned out to be false; there are now four living Shakers, with no new constituents pending.

Ludd's final bomb failed to go off; for two weeks it sat on a university campus, in the mailroom of a biology department. In reports to the media, more than a half-dozen students said they remembered picking up the package and moving it. The addressee, a professor conducting research in Ghana, was located and flown home by the federal government. Later this man would enjoy minor fame for being part of the first team of scientists to successfully clone a zebra.

All of Ludd's parcels were sent the same winter, mailed from Roseau, Minnesota. The postal clerk, a woman I'd known by name, recalled Ludd clearly and easily. Capped in each pipe shaft with match heads and gunpowder were the hooves of wild animals, broken to shards and then sharpened, so that upon detonation the things Ludd had killed would in turn go on to kill others.

My last month at the lake the weather was gorgeous: warm, and with little humidity. Each dawn, birdsong spilled from the wood. It stayed light to near ten in the evening. Families arrived with bright rubber rafts tied to the roofs of their station wagons. Mornings I fished from the shore near my porch, careful to keep my shadow behind me.

With my lease up and truck packed I went over to Ludd's, to tell him goodbye and say thank you. He'd asked little from me and offered a lot, and it's rare to find those sorts of people. A wooden Dutch door stood in the cabin's back wall; I'd knocked on it more with each season. I wouldn't say we were friends but a rapport had developed; we'd accepted each other as neighbors.

When Ludd answered that day there were nicks on his cheeks – he'd shaved his beard off completely. His jawline was short, his chin near to his lips. To say he looked different wouldn't be quite enough; some crucial part of him had seemed to go missing.

'Beard's gone,' I said.

'Summer,' Ludd answered. Bags wrapped his brown eyes. His girth spanned the frame of the doorway. Behind him, the cabin's interior was dark; the structure had been built without windows. From the room's depths issued the noise of Ludd's radio. In place of the singing I'd so often heard were only the sounds of raw frequency, a low wash of static out of which climbed a high-pitched metallic sort of chirping. I realized this to be the component's transmitter, searching for a signal and failing.

'I'm leaving tomorrow. I'm moving away,' I told him. Ludd held out his hand and I took it in mine. His long fingers crept up past my wrist bone. 'Okay,' he said, then let go and shut the door. It was the last time that I ever saw him.

The next morning I found the note on my porch. Ludd's handwriting was precise and looked very feminine, and at first I was confused about where the piece of paper had come from. What Ludd had left me was a quote by Thoreau, out of *Walden*:

> *A lake is the landscape's most beautiful and expressive feature. It is Earth's eye; looking into which the beholder measures the depth of his own nature.*

Today, the lake is no longer a lake; it was drained, and then used as landfill. Its image and name appear on no maps. There isn't any water to swim in. The country needed somewhere to bury its trash, and the area fit these requirements. Gone too are the cabins, Ludd's and my own, along with all of the others. The land's still protected, is still state land, there's just been a change in what's being guarded.

They never found Ludd; they searched and they searched. They dredged the lake then went north into Canada, a phalanx of men in navy-blue windbreakers moving over the earth and the nettles. A hotline was opened, bloodhounds employed. I watched it all on my TV in Beaumont. I've been down in the bayou for nearly two decades. I'm the owner of a rig diving outfit. For good money my shop gives scuba tours of the oil platforms just off the Gulf Coast. I've had a nurse shark swim nose first into the small of my back. I've found raw pearls at the bottom of the ocean.

I'm sure that he's dead, that Ludd took his own life or

that some act of nature – a rockslide, pneumonia – took it from him. But there is also a small part of me that believes that if I returned to the north I could find him, or rather that Ludd would somehow find me, that he would emerge from the woods with long hair and his beard, rifle slung over his shoulder. If we were to meet, though, I don't know what might happen next.

It's winter now, and I see the loons often.

EDGE BOYS

Bought in motel rooms, in public-park bathrooms, the edge boys have highlighted their hair. The boxes of Clairol are plucked stolen from shelves and tucked into boxer-brief waistbands. The store clerks are busy asking for price checks. The edge boys have very white teeth. They stride the linoleum, smiles shining out. The clerks think: no one that pretty would take things. The doors whoosh to open; here is the sun, here is the blacktop, shimmering. The edge boys wear shorts that go past their knees. The edge boys wear oversized T-shirts. They buy gum at gas stations and pace the grass strips between pump bays and street intersections. When cars slow in passing, the edge boys blow bubbles. Tucked in their anklets are pre-packaged condoms. They have earrings in both of their ears. Last week was the last week of their high-school semesters. The edge boys are ready to earn. In parentless houses, the kitchen tap running, they work water down to their scalps. Blond with red streaks or brown with blond streaks or black transformed to white blond. They wrap the dyed locks in lengths of tinfoil and wait watching game-show reruns. Their yearbooks, in backpacks, sit signed and forgotten: *have a great summer. i'll see you in autumn. thanks for being such a good friend.* The edge boys are gay. The edge boys have girlfriends, meek girls with glasses or cheeks stained with acne, who hide their girth under loose batik skirts, girls who ask less per their sub-par aesthetic and thus function as near-perfect foils, the edge boys needing only to take them to movies, to malls, to infrequently dine them at some neoned franchise and then later take their clothes off, this last part disliked but under-stood as essential, as requisite for the upkeep of hetero façade, mandatory for avoiding all manner of bullshit in locker-walled, fluorescent-lit halls, so these girls' hands held in high-ceilinged lunchrooms, these girls taken to prom, their taffeta dresses like bright shiny sacks, their matching slingbacks rubbing their fat ankles raw, and the edge boys make clear on spring nights in late April that it has been fun but just not enough, that it's in both parties' best interests to move on from each other, to let summer heal wounds and meet up in fall, and by the week after finals the edge boys are working, are putting in hours, are taking their knocks, have had their foreheads put hard against corners of nightstands, have been bruised by closed fists, have been robbed, have been taken to dark lonely lots off the parkways, the mood changing, the date going wrong, and sometimes the edge boys flee into night-time, hoping their sneakers don't scuff, as the body in youth will start itself over, can reset with nearly no flaws, but the shoes are expensive, were purchased, must last, possess sharp lines and clean looks, traits that the edge boys must also possess so the skin tanned in backyards on slow afternoons, the teeth brushed and whitened and flossed, the hair kept to flawless, shampooed and then sculpted, the back tightly tapered, sharp as the bristles on a brush – their image rechecked in the bathrooms of Chevrons as the day turns itself into dusk, and when the dye fades the edge boys repeat the process of dyeing, and when cars stop the edge boys lean through the frames of car windows, asking for rides to some other place, asking how much and for what.

And here the edge cities, the car-fervent boomburbs, Levittown's sprawling kempt spawn, more jobs than bedrooms, the streets dead by evening, the office parks sleeping it off; here the coiffed glow of post-industrial society, the middle class outsourced, the farmlands paved over, gone, practical know-how no longer important so goodbye to Pittsburgh's Steelworkers Union, goodbye to Baltimore's docks, the stevedores half-starved from nothing exported, the labor halls places of rot, production supplanted by codified knowledge, the making of goods replaced by the selling thereof, the old urban centers unwanted, not needed, high crime and high rent, the drug-addled dozing at bus stops, so development set down in between freeways, acreage near airports bought cheap and built up, and from this Bethesda and Scottsdale and Reston, Irving, Texas and White Plains, New York, here Costa Mesa in LA's choked basin, here Downer's Grove and Ogden, Utah, here the mid-level skyscraper of mixed office/retail, the arterial road ten miles long, where sidewalks are largely parachronistic as sidewalks are *places of sloth*, made for the beggar and stroller, the uncertain, the person too full of free thought, for the edge cities are kingdoms of the *action efficient*, progress optimized, apologism constantly scoffed – realms of the stem cell, the spreadsheet, the lepton, where the hum of the lathe has never been heard, where absent is the din of the die-caster's punch, these sounds replaced by the light constant clacking of flesh on computer keyboards, the new assembly lines well-lit partitioned desk cubicles one floor up from the whirr of juice bars, and rolled out from these factories datum not item, patent not part, as the things we make now are not things at all, are service or research, advice or idea, theory mapped out or thought up – here Science unbridled, here plugs, cords and wires, here bits, bytes and pixels replacing the orchards, all produce imported by plane and then truck, here nanotech labs with federal contracts, here the cybernetics start-up, *here green even sod between rows of parked cars outside the Mall of America*; here wetlands demolished, here cell towers erected, here all the bees dying off, here bigger and faster and smaller and brighter, here the twenty-screen Cineplex showing ten action titles, teens texting on hand-helds through all the slow parts, here drive-thru windows on pharmacy walls, here Zoloft and Lustral passed out like fast food, here tax breaks enormous for new corporate tenants, here regional outlets inside megacenters, here firms expert in hedge fund investment and intellectual property law; here unclassified research in the hills east of Berkeley, Houston's Sugarland, Denver's Aurora, here Cool Springs between Memphis and Nashville, here Clearwater due west of Tampa, each place a nexus of post-war success, these cities we fought for, these cities we won.

The edge boys do oral. The edge boys do anal. The edge boys will do half and half. On laptops, in bedrooms, listings are posted, published to websites with classified sections accepting of this sort of fare. The edge boys were born 1990 or after. The edge boys can type very fast. Cross-legged on throw rugs, on low thread-count bed sheets, the edge boy's shoulders hunch over flat screens, searching for what to say next. When their eyes blink, the edge boys don't know that they're blinking. On walls are taped posters of rock bands or rap stars or harmonizing Caucasian quintets. Square fans fill windows, their blades quickly turning. The rooms of the edge boys are never a mess. The rooms of the edge boys are kept swept and dusted, clothes hampered, corners absent of lint – quick work that functions as high-gloss veneer should parents, at some point, peek in. The edge boys do poorly on standardized testing; for them, it will be junior college at best. There is flash on the brainpan and their bodies hunch tighter and their fingers, crookedly, tap: *versatile bottom seeks high-class encounter. tan toned and ready right now. if you have the quarters come see my arcade. i have the best games in town.* The edge boys review; the edge boys make edits. The edge boys are junk food, sweet, cheap and addictive, so the edge boys call themselves twinks. With driveways vacated, with the highways now humming, with the sun burning dew from the grass, the edge boys are mid-morning entrepreneurs, undertaking new enterprise, assuming all risk. The edge boys are merchant fleet, caravan, troupe. The edge boys are both song and dance. The edge boys offer companionship, not fucking: *any money exchanged is a gift for time spent.* Pictures are uploaded alongside the squibs, photographic self-portraits in which the edge boys are shirtless, their faces made blurry or blacked out, as the edge boys must show what they have to offer without revealing too much of themselves. A lawnmower whirrs; cars honk a street over. Hummingbirds hover inches from blossoms; the edge boys can see them through cracks in the blinds. Light falls in threads onto desktops and dressers. The rooms of the edge boys are often so still that the edge boys sometimes believe themselves dead. From hallways chime wall clocks; it's seconds past ten. Windows are closed out and email then opened and soon after the ads of the edge boys go live. The edge boys stand up and step out of sweatpants. The edge boys own phony IDs – crude fakes they self-publish on laser-jet printers while their parents, exhausted, succumb to canned laughter on primetime TV – as the edge boys must be young-looking but legal, twenty-one, twenty, nineteen, some age that confirms them as virile and nubile but rules out anything statutory, and with music put on and their wardrobe selected, the edge boys walk briskly to white-tiled bathrooms, where towels hang folded in halves, the shower knob pulled out or turned right or left, the steam rising over the basin's glass door, the wall mirror growing fogged in.

And here the respondents, the white-collar lustful, alumni of Schools of Letters & Science, men in their twenties, their thirties, their fifties, men of all races and sizes, men who were born on American soil and men who at one point were naturalized, men who have been with the company for decades and men only recently hired, men who lean left and men who lean right and swing-voting men who will cross party lines should they really believe in the candidate, men with no voting record, men who watch sports ten hours each weekend and men who do not own a television, men who ride Harleys and men who drive hybrids; dumb men who will not last through the next round of lay-offs and men who are workers upstanding, men who wear suits with ties Windsor-knotted, men who wear lab coats and bow ties, men who are lead-end application designers and men who had once worked on Wall Street, men with full knowledge of the Doha Round's implications and men unsure of where Doha is located, men with low tolerance for processing lactose, men allergic to peanuts, to buckwheat; bearded men, bland men, men with thin fingers, men who are wearers of rings, men with tan lines where these rings once were but most aptly *men of duplicity*, men of the mask worn under the skin, men of coarse acts and good hygiene, men at once members of neighborhood-watch groups and blackguards for their local sex industry, and these men of the condo, the town house, the Tudor, these men of argyle and khaki, who stay late or rise early and work hard or don't, all of these men double-dealing – men of two forms, two positions in space, makers of both song and painting, men who are crooners of stanzas threnodic, peddlers of anapest, of trochee, men who know which sounds to stress and not stress to sell fables in a manner convincing: men of the midday trip to the dentist, men of cars whose oil needs changing, men who are fathers of very sick children, small boys or girls who abruptly fall ill at desks inside school buildings, and these children needing care, needing parent and transport, needing warm soup and cold remedies, so grave faces worn while approaching co-workers, or bosses in the middle of emailing: *I just got a call from, You won't believe this, He said* and *She said* and *Well they just told me* – lines near-canonical for each of these men, these scholars entrenched in the oral tradition of lying, as the edge boys are canvas that can't be left blank, are these men's passion, their calling, what they would choose if there was nothing else, no yard work, no anniversaries, no pushing of paper or processing words to sustain and increase yearly salary, so all manner of untruth composed and conscripted, the devotion to craft close to boundless, and here is the cell phone purchased in secret, and here the bank account no one else knows of, and here the PO box for these bills and statements, rented the next city over, as the lunch breaks of these men do not involve food but do very much include *hunger*, so daily or weekly, in the stalls of work bathrooms, or in cars parked in the dark of garages, the ads of the edge boys perused via BlackBerry, flipped through using touch-screens on iPhones, and when the right hue is found, the precise chiaroscuro, these men then envision their paintings: art made amongst cheaply starched sheets of queen beds in rooms advertised as having free cable, or the bought trysts transpiring well into evening, subject and object in states of undress at rest stops on the city's periphery, and sometimes the process goes very smoothly and on occasion the practice is rougher, but more important than outcome *sustained feasibility*, that these actions are able to be tried and retried, to be done again over and over.

The edge boys want their donation up front. The edge boys take cash and cash only. The edge boys will wear any items you like, providing they then get to keep them. The edge boys can tell you which parts of lots can't be seen from the street, from the freeway. The edge boys don't ever kiss on the mouth though the men that they meet *will lean in*, will keep trying, and by now, my mid-forties, still married, still scared, still fake small meek and unsure, a member of gyms, a father of daughters, as someone who dishonored oath long ago but has largely upheld every contract, as owner of a house now fully paid off, as possessor of matching brass shoehorns, as someone who never stood up for himself and finds richness in acts done in shadow, in darkness, the edge boys, for me, serve as *opera omnia*, comprise a life's work collected, and here early works: my third year at Lehigh, a major in civil engineering, freshly admitted to Tau Beta Pi and possessed by the deeds of Telford, of Jessop, both pre-eminent builders of canals, of artificial channels of water, this '83, Rock Hudson infected, the disease often still called gay cancer, AIDS known to Regan who was two years away from using the term while in public, and *winter in Bethlehem*, bright but cold days, the steel plant still up and running, the historic downtown lined with bare elms, the clothiers and bookshops brick-walled and stately, and for ten months by this time letters to parents, verse that spoke often of Daphne: Daphne of Cleveland, Daphne a senior, Daphne who too soon was graduating, and included therein our fake union's minutiae, trips to Ohio or north to the Catskills or hikes to the top of South Mountain, the posts detailed but also disjointed, meant to seem rushed, to seem done in one breath, to convey I was in constant hurry, whereas in truth there was only coursework and near-daily walks, done close to sunset, down to the bank of the river, brisk peregrinations from my Fountain Hill in-law past one side of St Luke's Memorial, where often a nurse, in pink scrubs and pea coat, stood smoking by a low bank of generators, and with eye contact made and a quick nod hello his shoe tramps on the dirt path behind me, and these men my seniors by a decade or more – there were eight in two years, in total – and while I remember their faces and where they said they grew up and the deep grove of white pines we went to, I cannot recall a single one of their names or if they once ever told their names to me, but nonetheless closeness, something near respite, relief from a bleak way of seeing, as while I adored all the things human beings had made I mainly despised human beings: saw their design as short-sighted, their construction haphazard, their maintenance needing too much maintaining, but hidden by trees, dusk sinking to night, *the singing of near-perfect industry*, here pressure and density, here equations of state, here balance, breath measured, entropic, and when we were finished, had switched ourselves off and parted from each other's company, within me was calm, flat neutral and static, the job done, the stars still indifferent, and so over time, and through acts of this manner, I came to see love as *duty to work*, a viewpoint not that uncommon, as I held great affection for accomplishing a task, for procedure done forthwith and fitly, and by May of my last year in North Appalachia, that region of limestone and sinkholes, I knew I would always live two lives at once, a life seen and a life more invisible, and knew also that these lives would transpire in parallel, would move forward in space at a similar rate while remaining at all points equidistant, but ignored in this thinking *Euclidean principle*, as according to Euclid on a spherical plane all straight lines are turned into circles, bend warp and wrap, are bound by their globe, and thereby become geodesic, and with Earth a sphere this meant points intersecting, meant contact made between two different things that I'd thought I could always keep separate.

And here mid-career, the Near North Side loft, my wife holding a torn condom wrapper, the two of us poised on opposite sides of our kitchen's marble-topped island, light pouring in through the balcony's sliding glass doors, reflecting from off of Lake Michigan, this '97, the boom in full swing, the country choking on money, and with one arm akimbo the person I married releasing the ripped piece of plastic, the object suspended and then falling slowly to the smooth beige Biancone counter, and on this woman's wrist a chain of white gold, and on her finger a ring of white diamonds, and the condom itself, once contained in the wrapper, in a trashcan at Anna Page Park west of Rockford, used in conjunction with a junior in high school, a boy named Brandon O'Cleary, taller than average and lithe and light-haired and dressed in grunge-era trappings: ripped jeans and cloth high-tops and plaid flannel shirts, worn despite the damp heat of deep summer, button-down items undone by myself on at least ten separate occasions, the two of us coming to know one another per work for the firm that employed me, endeavors involving repeated site visits to dozens of area cities, as these places were ready to take on more people, were building hundreds and hundreds of houses, and along with these houses new schools and boutiques and plazas and fire departments, structures intended to be flanked by small ponds, by fountains and banks of bright flowers, and lawns would be needed and toilets and bath-tubs and all this depended on *water*, as without water no dwellers could dwell, and no shoppers could do all their shopping, and no roads would be tarred and no sprinklers would hiss and the juice bars would have no crushed ice for their smoothies, so watershed checked for all type of pollutants, farmland surveyed for new aquifers, and here's where to pipe in to existing storm drains and here's how to maintain water tables – all of this data determined and gauged, collected for further analysis, and at night in hotel rooms in Schaumburg or Elgin calls home to the woman I married: *I'm just checking in* and *Yes things are fine* and *I can't wait to get home and see you,* sayings which in some ways were not utter lies as I loved my wife then and I still do, but with the receiver set down on its cream-colored base a walk to my car to start *trolling,* cruising each village – the malls and gas stations – for boys who were in need of money, who were willing to part with one type of resource in order to then gain another, as I wanted something both soulless and lissome and the edge boys had this to offer, could promise me dividend with low overhead if I was willing to become a partner, and at tables in food courts not far from arcades or in restrooms out west toward the toll roads, the edge boys and I would come to terms quickly, as we were living within a bull market, and yes there were blips – a kidney infection, a stop at a DUI checkpoint – but the tech bubble was big and said bubble was growing and past the continued growth rate of this bubble few other things seemed to matter, so *repeated foray* while my wife sat at home with first one and then both of our children, and the paychecks were big and I had money in blue chips and things just kept growing and growing, and the first of our daughters grew out of her onesies and went to her first day of preschool, and the suburbs expanded, spawned acres of homes, replete with skylights and bird feeders, where young men and women, the moon overhead, supplemented their own genealogy, while beneath them new pipes pushed out all their sewage, carried their waste to wherever, but what I mean to say is there was no need to think, only an urge to keep doing, so when the condom's torn wrapper touched down on the counter I looked at my wife very calmly, crossed my arms on my chest and leveled my eyes and explained that conference in Denver, where by true chance I ran into someone that I knew from my days back at Lehigh, and her name was Daphne and she was from Cleveland and one drink had led to three others – and the story was seamless (there were parts told while weeping), and I beseeched my wife not to leave me, to accept my mistake and think of our daughters and think of the concept of family, something that I, for one night of my life, had so foolishly placed by the wayside; and while this tale was spun into something metallic, into something expensive and shiny, my thoughts went again, as they still sometimes do, to the image of Brandon O'Cleary, his long body leaning on a tall granite wall littered with crooked graffiti, his hair to mid-ear, deep blond and unwashed and parted straight down the middle, the locks grimy enough to keep a clean angle, to roof his face in an A-frame, and Brandon liked music and Brandon liked pot and Brandon liked shooting home movies, and set up his parents' bulky camcorder on a tripod each Sunday evening, where before dusk and until shortly after he filmed from his small bedroom's window, the lens looking down the length of his street, looking, he told me, at *nothing*, at cars leaving driveways and children on bikes, at snowfall and rainfall and hail, and stacked in his closet were columns of tapes, some years old and some very recent, these acts of surveying disclosed to me while I set up my firm's total station, a device that like Brandon's sat too on a tripod, and was also used in surveying, and when Brandon approached and said what the hell is that I told him of angles and distance, of sight via prisms and data recording and how to look under and over and straight through the Earth, how to see measure test and tell everything.

But now it is summer and I've rushed through my life, only to find other summers, more seasons of heat, double-headers and picnics, more evenings of lush thrumming stillness, more weeks of monotonous unchallenging work, more checks written for property taxes, more vacations taken to mundane locales: lighthouses or churches or statues or bridges, trips now made most often without me, my wife and two daughters wanting time to themselves, a concept I don't find surprising, as while I've been a good father in a number of ways I am also quite guilty of distance, of supporting my offspring with money, not love, of remaining emotionally absent, a shortcoming my spouse has said she equates to our children being not male but female, that I have had a hard time accepting my role in our family and that from this our family suffers, but when they pack up the Jeep for points west or east there is, within me, real sadness, deep melancholy that I've failed at my task, that I couldn't perform any better, that on car rides to St Louis to lay eyes on the Arch or to Wyoming to hike in the Tetons, I am spoken of poorly – not called spiteful names in tones bright with rage but wondered at, frowned upon, questioned, the way the favored team's fans, having watched their club lose, leave the stadium bewildered and empty: *They should have done better* and *What were they thinking?* and to provide counterbalance to these feelings of shame I walk to my den and computer, boot up the hard drive and sit down at my chair and see who is working this evening, who will meet me at street corners close to the mall, where the big summer sale is happening, where nightly the blacktops, like still inland seas, wait for the next day's sojourners, temporary residents of these declining Edens, as America is reaching its summer, that point where all bloom has happened, where what has sprung from the earth shows off what it's got and waits patiently for *decomposition*: the peaking of oil, the drying of rivers, the crops lying wrecked in their rows in the heartland or some other crippling paucity, and for this reason the edge boys are genuine artifact, Americana that's highly collectible, each one like the last one but also unique, made individual via small details: a birthmark or scar or small discoloration, a type of deodorant whose scent is brand new to me, a way of dyeing their hair that I'd never thought of or a piercing in some place that I had not seen, and on these evening drives to the malls or motels, I allow myself time to wander my city, take in each billboard and juice bar and gas pump, every neon, glowing marquee, and here is the semi just in from the freeway, its trailer filled with plasma TVs, and here the grease franchise, burgers and shakes, cars ringing three sides of the building, the doors locked but the drive-thru window still open, its panes retracting hydraulically, and farther out from town landfill and power plants and all manner of *infrastructure unsightly* – squat concrete structures where sewage is treated, as the clean must be kept from the dirty.

And Brandon, my favorite, do they know what their acts bring, these people of cities on the edges of cities? Do they know that all this is ending? That how things are now are not how they will be? That this grand experiment's over? That the Fed has cut rates per blowback from subprime and still these places are failing? That homes being built now will never be lived in? That at the auto plazas, units aren't moving? That people work longer than ever before and earn less than they did at mid-century? That the petals have dried out and the stalks are all rotting? Because, Brandon, I know it, and this is why last night I put in my two weeks after being telephoned by a headhunter, an anonymous man two time zones away representing a firm working in *catastrophe modeling*, in the scientific prediction of disaster, in detailing what type of wrath to expect when the next hurricane descends on the Gulf Coast, or the big one arrives to shake down San Francisco, or the southwest has its next batch of fires, or the Singapore Causeway succumbs to tsunami or a flood eats some county in Kansas, for these events, now, are just short of certain, and insurers want to cover their asses – need to know what kind of odds are in play, if gross loss will be millions or billions, and for this *computer-assisted scenarios*, software eschatological in nature, programs designed to map out the End Times second by second by second, and here's what to expect when the Bay Bridge collapses, and here's what this zip code will look like as rubble, and here's what turns to ash if winds blow from the west as opposed to blowing northwesterly and, Brandon, the money's terrific, the sum offered much more than I would have expected for my input on our slow apocalypse, and for this reason I will again move my daughters and wife, and will sell my house and then buy a new house, and find yet another tree-lined tranquil street in a newly made master community, where each house looks just like the last one, some split-level in which I may hide a bit longer and wait while things turn truly sour, for coastlines to shrink and shelves to go bare and gas to hit twenty a gallon, and perhaps I won't ever see it, will expire before we fully lose balance, and fall from our perch on the roof of the world, spiraling downward and downward, and it was to be different, *there were to be bluebirds*, there were to be grills near the shore of a lake, a post-war aria of infinite refrain; we were to applaud, and be applauded. There was the promise of promise. We had solved something. The dead were brought back from French beaches and honored. The dollar held. Wheat grew. We made things of substance. But it all went perverted, we purchased each other, and we left you, Brandon, with nothing, with hair dye and game shows and modified food, with the ghost of Social Security, with lead in the paint on the walls of your schools, with electromagnetic pollution, with esplanades of red brick where the hollow walk shopping, the headsets of their cell phones like blinders, with some small bit of wealth that can never make up for the damage inflicted upon you and, Brandon, I'm sorry, I should have known better, I should have made more prudent choices, but what I loathe most about the person I am is also the thing that completes me so, Brandon, please, one kiss, I'm done asking, we have financialized your humanity, we have taken and taken, and there's no stopping this and there's no cure for this and so coated in fear, lust and haste are our happenings that we forget wholly *implication*, that these cities, like rash on the skin of the land, are symptomatic of more dire virus, and once in a host will not go away but replicate over and over and, Brandon, my pet, we're low on vaccine, and the antibiotics are useless, and small bits of plastic float in our seas, debris no bigger than plankton, sharp brittle shards that won't biodegrade, not now and not ever – are proof we were here, in our miserable way, have washed up on every island, and wrecked every acre and nautical mile, and spun the hand on our moral compass, and without any pride or belief in ourselves exist without any power, and supplanting this *war*, and replacing this *purchase*, as we give ourselves over to skirmish and item, and our guilt gels around us, forms into things that we can't escape so more things are built to contain them, and if we don't like how they look they can always be brightened so, Brandon, keep bleaching, burn through every root, because if you're not pretty then you'll get no money, and if you don't feed us, we promise, we'll eat you.

NYCTICORAX
NYCTICORAX

Gus Bender was heading south on County Route 55, his Ag-Chem 3104 Terra-Gator at full speed, twenty miles an hour, on the road's shoulder. Two pistons were firing rough and the mechanics would no longer make house calls, the shop having been bought by a larger company and changing their policy, so Gus, on his Saturday, was now driving the thirty miles into town on a bad engine. He wasn't looking forward to the check he would be writing; one county over a farmer had reported the first case of soybean rust in the entire state of Iowa. The fungus made leaves drop early, stopping the pods from setting. If it spread to Gus's crops, he could lose half his yield or more. The only way to prevent outbreak was to spray with a new fungicide developed down in the Southern states, where the rust had made its way up from. The spray cost eighteen-eighty per gallon. Infestation or not, Gus would not earn this year. At best, he hoped to break even.

Gus looked up to the blue June sky. Some type of large bird was circling above him. He fiddled with the climate panel below the dashboard, trying to figure out how to turn the air off. The cab of the bright yellow Gator had a three-level environmental filtration system which meant, as far as Gus could tell, that he had no control over his environment at all. He'd bought the model in Council Bluffs two months earlier, after the plant in Jackson, Minnesota had stopped making parts for the three-wheel applicator he'd had since Ford was in office. On the sales floor a college kid in a collared shirt had talked to him about multi-duct heating and the air-ride captain's chair. All Gus had wanted to know was if the engine was low-maintenance.

'What you're looking at is the very latest in off-road vehicles for the application of biosolids, manure and other dewatered organic residuals,' the kid told Gus, reading from a clipboard.

'So you can't answer my question, or you won't?' asked Gus. The two of them were standing in a glass-walled showroom with forty-foot ceilings. Gus thought it was the type of place where they should be selling European sedans, not farm equipment.

'I know there's an onboard computer that regulates tire pressure,' the teenager offered. 'I know you've got three color options to choose from.'

'I know if a tire is getting low and I don't care about color options,' said Gus. 'Now what can you tell me about the engine?'

'We can look at the specs on that, for sure,' the kid said, nodding and flipping through the clipboard's pages. His hair was bleached blond and slathered with gel. The tips stood up like the tines of a fork. The boy was tan the way people on television were: a bronze that was almost an orange. Gus let the air out of his lungs. He spent the following hour discussing financing options with the dealership's manager. Gus had near a decade's worth of monthly installments until the machine would be paid off in full. It had occurred to him that he might expire before such a thing happened.

A black Pontiac sped by the Terra-Gator, close enough that the driver almost took his car's mirror off. Gus smashed his palm down on the Terra-Gator's horn. From under the hood came a sound like a doeling in labor. The Terra-Gator weighed as much as a dump truck – more in the fields, with its sprayers attached. Each tire was five feet tall. Gus watched the Pontiac's driver-side window roll down, a man's arm extending to the elbow. With the bird flapping overhead Gus stared at the man's raised middle finger, the digit growing smaller as the car sped off down the blacktop.

Iowa's latest state slogan was 'Fields of Opportunities', and Dick Bradsky's business trip was turning out to be just that. He couldn't believe how cheap the land was, or how little he had to do to get its owners to part with it.

For two days he'd come west from Chicago in a cherry-red rented Mustang, the land-appraisal firm of Wiley Associates footing the bill for Dick's trip to the counties around Council Bluffs, to meet with farmers looking to dump acreage for cents on the dollar. Dick was low-rung on the corporate ladder and his office buddies, Baker and Nichols, had scoffed when he'd drawn assignment to the western side of the Hawkeye State, to evaluate useless land in the middle of nowhere. The three of them had gone out to a steakhouse after work last Tuesday, finishing three rounds of Martinis in forty-five minutes and growing giggly from the alcohol. When the waitress had asked if they were ready to order, Dick had stared exactly at her chest and said he would like the baked potatoes. This had made Baker and Nichols laugh to the point of sobbing.

'All the fixin's,' Dick had added, as the waitress stormed off.

He'd spent his first night on the road at the Hilton in Des Moines, possibly the least charming city on the planet, though his escort, a pretty if overweight blonde named Mitzi, spoke very highly of it. On the phone, the yellow pages spread over his lap, Dick had told her an extra fifty was in it if she arrived with a large pizza, deep-dish, in an hour or less.

'Like that one commercial!' Mitzi had said with enthusiasm.

'You betcha!' Dick had replied, hanging up as he unbelted his dress slacks.

His motel room in Treynor, Iowa, two hours southwest of the capital, looked like the 1970s had crawled from hell and was resting. The bathroom wallpaper was striped orange and white, with gold starbursts exploding all over it. The main room's carpet was mustard-yellow shag. In the wood-paneled lobby Dick had asked the clerk where a good place to eat dinner might be. He was sure he had seen the woman on one of those television shopping networks, modeling fashions for the female husky.

'We got a Friendly's and a Country Kitchen and a Checker's,' the clerk said. 'And they opened a KFC in the gas station down the road last month.'

'That's super,' Dick said. 'So much to choose from.'

'What gets you here from Chicago?' the clerk asked. She had taken a long time looking at Dick's license when he had checked in, like the words there were code she might break shortly.

'Work,' Dick told the woman. 'I'm here on business.'

'That so? And what's a man like yourself do?'

'I appraise eminent domain.'

The woman gave Dick a wide, clueless smile. 'That's like computers and stuff, right?' she asked.

'That's it exactly,' Dick said, nodding slowly and earnestly. '*You* are a very smart woman.'

Dick had spent the next two days, Thursday and Friday, out in the cut, driving to acreages and meeting with men who had ventured beyond their zip code's boundaries perhaps as often as once. Wiley Associates made their money on seeing the bigger picture in regard to land seizure, where so many other people could not. In a polite and professional tone, Dick assured grizzled farmer after grizzled farmer that while Wiley would indeed be purchasing their land, they had no plans whatsoever to develop on it. What Dick failed, repeatedly, to mention, was the next step in the firm's process, where Wiley sold the land to the highest corporate or governmental bidder. Farmer Bob could keep on with his fields, until the state felt like putting power lines through them, or a contractor was ready to break ground on a mall. There were other considerations, too: subsurface easements for pipelines, air rights for bridges and planes. What Wiley Associates and Dick understood very well was that land was utterly finite, and sooner or later every square inch of it would be highly sought after, even southwest Iowa's. Especially southwest Iowa's.

In two days Dick had closed five deals and was ready for a return to a viable urban center. He stopped at the Friendly's and bought five one-hundred-dollar gift certificates, one for each of the families he had swindled. Such gestures, Dick knew, were like spells to the people of the heartland. After dropping off the last of these, however, and giving his final bullshit handshake, Dick had gotten himself lost.

On the county roads a wrong turn became two, then more. The intersections offered no street signs, only guesswork. The battery of Dick's cell phone had gone dead, its charger in a desk drawer in Treynor. The Mustang's gas gauge dipped under a quarter. Dick backtracked through dust brought up by his own tires. Everything looked exactly the same but nothing looked familiar: there were only crops and farmhouses and more crops. To calm himself Dick thought about the future, looking ahead to that time when the glaciers and ice caps really got melting and the rising oceans shrank the coasts, when San Francisco and Miami and Houston were submerged forever and people packed into the country's middle, building skyscrapers amongst the corn stalks. In the distance Dick watched a bird making circles in the June air.

'I own what you're flying in,' Dick told the bird. 'Pay up.'

Gibby Swain is having a conversation with Satan at the small table in the middle of his grandmother's kitchen. Centered on a white plate in front of Gibby is an egg-salad sandwich. The table's Formica top is the same color as the egg mixture, which is also the same color as the room's walls. Gibby is sixteen years old and hasn't slept in four days. In the high-school parking lot last Tuesday he had given three fifty-dollar bills, his birthday money, to a Chinese drug dealer from Omaha. In return the drug dealer had given him ten grams of methamphetamine, in a sealed baggie with a skull-and-crossbones print on it. The small thing had looked so full Gibby thought it was going to pop.

'That's a cool-looking baggie,' Gibby had said.

'I was never here,' said the drug dealer, then drove off in his sleek white Acura.

Gibby was trying to remember the man's name, though currently Gibby was having trouble remembering things, like what was real and what was not. For example, Gibby was pretty sure that either Satan or the egg-salad sandwich was real, but not both. Behind Gibby, at the kitchen sink, his eighty-four-year-old grandmother was chopping carrots.

The speed, Gibby knew, was most certainly real. He had finished off the last of it at dawn, tearing the bag open along its seam and rooting at the crystals stuck to the plastic with his tongue. It was Saturday and soon Gibby would be expected to mow the front lawn. Past the kitchen's single window he could feel the grass growing, each blade getting taller. *Murderer*, the blades announced through the pane glass, *murderer*.

Gibby blinked and tiny silver explosions appeared on the crusts of the egg-salad sandwich. Satan had taken a break from talking but was still looking at him. He was bright red and dressed in a red cape, had hooves for feet, a black goatee, and thick black glasses. Goat horns sprouted from the top of his head. Gibby thought Satan looked a little like his algebra teacher, Mr Nester, after he had come back sunburned from a trip to California.

'Do you want some?' Gibby said, sliding the plate with the egg-salad sandwich in Satan's direction.

'That's for you,' said Gibby's grandmother. 'I already had one.' Gibby watched Satan mouth these words at the exact pace that his grandmother said them. She spoke in slow motion, her syllables garbled; Gibby thought she sounded like one of those witnesses whose faces they blacked out on *America's Most Wanted*. Chop-chop, chop-chop, went the knife through the carrots. Gibby wondered what his grand-mother could be doing with so many carrots. It seemed like she had been chopping for decades, a lifetime, since before his parents had died and he had come to live with her. Gibby could picture the pieces of carrot filling up the metal sink and spilling onto the floor's white linoleum, a veritable sea of carrots that Gibby would almost certainly drown in. Then, with startling clarity, Gibby realized what was going on.

'She's going to cook you,' said Satan, speaking Gibby's thought.

'Really?' asked Gibby. He was scratching ferociously at the insides of his arms.

'Yes,' said his grandmother. 'I'm stuffed at the moment but there's dinner to think about. And don't you forget to mow the lawn, Gibby. Work like that will put some meat on your bones.'

Chop-chop went the knife, chop-chop.

Gibby smoothed his hands over the front of his Black Sabbath *War Pigs* T-shirt then tucked his oily brown hair behind his ears. His ten-dollar Radio Shack Walkman had run out of batteries on the school bus yesterday afternoon. The blow had been crushing. Upon arriving home he'd stolen the double-As from the television controller but these too had run out on him. Gibby doubted if he would ever sleep again. He wanted to very badly but if he couldn't then he wanted to listen to some very heavy music, at a very loud volume, very soon in the future.

'There's a radio in her car,' said Satan, crossing a hoof over the opposite knee and pointing a long finger at Gibby's grandmother. 'You could sit in her car and listen to music there.'

'I don't know where the keys are,' said Gibby.

'They're in the bowl of caramels on top of her dresser,' said Satan. 'She hides them there.'

'No excuses,' said Gibby's grandmother.

'Because she knows I hate caramels,' Gibby whispered to his dining companion. Satan nodded carefully. His head started to melt then began boiling then reformed itself. The sandwich's white bread looked like foam rubber. Gibby thought this might be a good time to go get his chore taken care of.

The Terra-Gator was losing speed; Gus watched the gauge dip to twelve then ten miles an hour. The intersection of Highway 2 and County Road J was a hundred yards ahead. After that he had twenty miles to Treynor.

It was a beautiful June weekend and Gus wished badly he could be at home in the backyard, tending his small garden's perennials. Since his wife's death five years ago the garden had become both hobby and challenge, Gus having paid it little attention while Elizabeth had been alive. Their only child, Jason, was thirty years old. He lived in Atlanta with Thomas, his boyfriend. The two of them owned a pet shop.

Gus and his son had not spoken for some time. Jason had

left the state promptly after finishing college at Ames, telling his parents he had an offer in Georgia he couldn't pass up. He'd returned for Christmases and once over summers and then for Elizabeth's funeral, bringing the boyfriend, for the first time, along with him. Thomas was six-four and skinny and African-American. At the service he'd worn a blue blazer with no shirt and white leather pants. His face was wreathed in a thick beard but his head was shaved bald. Even the minister had stared in amazement.

In Gus's kitchen, during the reception, Thomas had offered condolences and a bright green gift bag containing a rhinestone collar for Ida, Gus's short-haired pointer.

'She doesn't wear a collar, she's a hunting dog,' Gus told Thomas. Elizabeth had died from a blood clot while gardening six days earlier. Walking in from the fields Gus had seen something spread out over the house's back lawn. He'd started running when he realized what it was.

From the living room, country music played softly on the radio. 'This is Merle Haggard, yes?' asked Thomas.

'That's right,' Gus said. 'I'm surprised you know that.'

'Because I'm black or because I'm gay?'

'Both,' said Gus.

'How's it going in here?' asked Jason, walking in and leaning against the refrigerator. He was holding a piece of celery he'd taken from the buffet table.

'About as well as expected,' said Thomas.

'Dad, we're going to go into town. Do you need anything?'

'There are still guests here, Jason.'

'Exactly, that's why we're leaving, right now.'

'You could have told me about this and not just shown up with him,' Gus said. 'It's your mother's funeral.'

'Family's important to me and Thomas,' said Jason, biting into the stick of celery. 'We're going to try to adopt soon, though we doubt seriously if the state will let us.'

Gus turned to consider his son. Jason had Elizabeth's long chin and narrow eyes and blonde hair. Gus's own mother, when she had been alive, had said how good this was, that getting the mother's traits meant the boy would turn out kind and learn to love the world. In his gray pinstriped suit and leather shoes, Gus thought Jason looked like he should be working on Wall Street, not sweeping feces out of cages in a pet shop.

'You're going to stay here until the guests leave,' Gus said.

'No,' Jason said, 'we're not.'

'Can you recommend a good place to dine at?' said Thomas. He was smirking at Gus and stroking his beard.

'I can recommend three places and if I were you I wouldn't hold hands in any of them,' Gus told his son's boyfriend.

'That's pretty much what I thought you would say,' said Thomas.

'Oh my God I can't believe this is happening,' Jason said.

'Neither can I,' said Gus.

Thomas and Jason had left shortly after, remaining absent

for the rest of the evening and leaving Gus alone in the empty house. They spent the next two nights at a hotel in Omaha, paying short visits mid-afternoons, when Jason knew Gus would be out in the fields. Both days they brought gift baskets of fruit and wrapped cheeses, along with unsigned store-bought sympathy cards. On the third day, they flew back to Atlanta.

For a month then more Gus had only kept working, numb from the shock of loss. Part of him felt like his son had died along with Elizabeth, that a single act had taken both of them from him at the very same moment.

'I'm your father,' Gus said, calling Jason on Thanksgiving, 'I offered you everything I could.' In the background he could hear Thomas singing in a fake country accent.

'Well it wasn't enough,' Jason said, then hung up.

The bird was in front of the Terra-Gator now, perhaps only ten feet above Gus. He could make out most of the animal's markings: a black back and white belly, gray wings and a long dark beak. Gus looked toward the Larson farm, derelict for the last three crop cycles. Gone also were the Hennings and the Groffs. Every year there were fewer lights on the horizon. At the point where the county road crossed the highway the Terra-Gator threw a rod, its wheels slowing to a stop. Gus climbed down from the vehicle's cab. From the north, a red car was approaching. Gus waited glumly on the edge of the highway.

* * *

On the back seat of the rented Mustang was a crumpled road map, Dick's sunglasses, snapped at their bridge, and the car's rear-view mirror, ripped down by Dick and banged repeatedly against the console's air vents until long cracks had appeared in the glass.

This last act of violence had occurred at the intersection of County Road Please and Rural Route Kill Me, Dick getting out of the Mustang and kicking the door's side panel and asking God why he needed to mock Dick always, why he had kept him out of all of the Northeast's top-tier business schools, why he'd made Dick fat and lonely and sad and had him project this fatness and sadness upon other people who were also fat and sad, why he'd trapped Dick in a rural death maze, far from everything, so distant that even Dick's pleadings to the deity that had abandoned him here would go unheard, removed as Dick was from anything resembling civilization.

The single piece of information Dick had been afforded by his out-of-car tantrum was the discovery of a long aluminum pole lying in the grass ditch beside the intersection – there were no street signs anywhere because someone had stolen all of them, had removed the markers on purpose, was playing a big funny joke.

Jokes had followed Dick like jackals throughout his life, since the very beginning. Obese from birth, his mother had spent eighteen hours getting Dick out of her, a fact that even now she repeated at family gatherings and holiday dinners, the tale of Dick's complicated and agonizing journey from the womb given Homeric qualities, turned to epic while Dick sat feet away. On the asphalt courts and grass playing fields of Evanston's public schools the name-calls became a sort of clothing, stitched and sewn by Dick's classmates, the patterns and styles more extravagant with every passing year. By high-school graduation Dick's esteem had shrunk to nothing; he bought bags of cookies the way alcoholics buy beer.

His roommate in college at Urbana had also been fat, the admissions board pairing the doomed with the doomed. Dick's peers' derision arrived indirectly, through acts of quiet exclusion. At parties he was a mute fused to a wall. All around him were boys he wanted to befriend, girls that he wanted to sleep with. The roommate, Brad Willard, unable to bear it, leapt from their third-story window during finals week, breaking bones in both legs and returning forever to Ohio. It became clear to Dick he would have to adapt to ensure his own survival.

So Dick began to tell jokes.

Dick bought books and watched stand-up and printed out lists of vulgar one-liners he found online. He practiced movement, timing, delivery, stance. At night, in bed, Dick repeated his material over and over, Brad Willard's stripped mattress staring out at him. The humors became a kind of prayer and soon Dick had memorized fifty, sixty, one hundred of them. In the dormitory's hallway bathroom Dick found a stage, offering up his aperçus at the rows of sinks or urinals whenever he had an audience.

I didn't sleep well last night, the cake store was cold.
I was going to go out but then Greenpeace showed up.
What's the difference between a tent and my shirt?
Nothing; nothing at all.

They were good or bad, smart or dumb, and somehow, somehow, they worked for Dick; they allowed people to include him. At dinners or bars he talked and they laughed, only now they laughed along with him. Dick learned the trick was keeping the gun pointed back at himself, to make sure each joke was grounded in self-deprecation. He spoke of what it was like growing up in a hog pen or in the sea, with the rest of the pod. He picked up bar tabs and bought rounds of pizzas. He was the ride to the airport, the shoulder to cry on, the sudden tutor, the last resort. Dick relished each title granted him, and through it all he told his jokes. Sometimes he was invited to sporting events by his new, earned friends; sometimes he managed encounters with the less desired females.

But Dick's efforts were never enough. He was still heavy, still a burden. From dorm food Dick put on more weight. He worked hard in school but fell short of straight As, the rigors of social acceptance distracting him. Columbia said no, then Yale, then Harvard. Brown and BU and Cornell followed suit. Again and still, Dick was unwanted. So it was back to Northwestern, to where he grew up, then a slew of corporate journeyman positions, the last of these sending him to Iowa.

Dick stood in the June air, breathing. His starched oxford shirt had untucked itself at the waist, the tails as creased as the skin on his stomach. When did it all end, he wondered, when did it stop? He got back in the car and turned over the engine, checking the rear-view, which wasn't there. Dick looked over his shoulder then pulled out onto the gravel road. Still ahead of him was the circling bird, dipping and rising. Dick decided to head for it, guessing it was a hawk or a falcon, some species that circled the highways and interstates, finding easy targets to pick off.

For the cassette player in his grandmother's Dodge Dart, Gibby has selected Metallica's first album, *Kill 'Em All*. The player's volume dial is turned up to maximum. The music has already blown out the front speakers. The guitars make Gibby smile uncontrollably. His jaw hurts from grinding his teeth.

Next to the driveway, on the lawn, is the mower. Its engine is still running; the long handle lies in the grass. Earlier, in the kitchen, Gibby had excused himself from the table and walked down the short hallway to the back of the house. His grandmother's bedroom looked like history had exploded: covering the floor were porcelain dolls and stacks of old newspapers, a brass gramophone and moldering copies of

Life. A narrow path wound through these items, to the twin bed and oak dresser against the far wall.

The keys had been where Gibby's lunch guest had said they would be, in the wide crystal bowl of caramels perched on the dresser's top. Beside the bowl was a framed photo of Gibby's parents; they had died in a chairlift accident while on a trip they'd won to Vermont. Gibby had been ten. Sometimes, in his mind, he could remember what they looked like. Other times, he could not.

Gibby had put the keys in his pocket and gone outside and pulled the mower from the sagging equipment shed. Before yanking the machine's ripcord, Gibby had bent close to the grass. 'It's your time,' he'd whispered. The blades trembled. Gibby blew air at them, smiled, and stood up.

Gibby's grandmother's car is apple green. The smell of the seats' white vinyl surrounds him. It is a pleasant smell. Gibby is very, very tired. He wishes he had more of the drugs he bought. Then, like a gift, he remembers. Gibby gets out of the car and walks to the mailbox at the end of the driveway. With one hand he opens the box's door and searches the inside of the metal roof. The pads of Gibby's fingers run over something smooth. Gibby finds a corner and pulls. The tape on either side of the small white envelope unfastens easily. Gibby opens the envelope. Inside are a note and a long stripe of pale yellow powder, resting in the envelope's seam. Gibby unfolds the note and reads it:

Gibby,

This is Gibby. If you're reading this, you've found the speed. Remember to never stop rocking, no matter what anyone tells you. I promise that you can always count on me.

Gibby walks back to the car thinking it is a good thing, having friends. *Kill 'Em All*'s second song, 'Four Horsemen', begins. Gibby gets in and shakes the powder onto the bench seat. The speed is only slightly darker than the seat's upholstery. Gibby searches the vinyl with his nose, like an aardvark scanning for ant holes. He locates every speck of powder. His nostrils burn and the world quickens. Gibby feels compelled to keep up with it.

He decides it is time to go driving.

Gibby has never driven a car before and getting out to the road poses difficulty. He turns the ignition and looks behind him, putting his foot down on the gas pedal. The car lurches forward, its grille hitting the gate that leads to the backyard. Gibby changes the gear to reverse. He thinks about his grandmother, her evil, subtle plans. She is virtually deaf and ignores the world beyond the house if she is not outside, in it. No meat for you tonight, grandmother, Gibby thinks. Leaving, he sideswipes the mailbox. Ahead of him is the same stretch of road he walks every weekday, two miles of gravel that connect to Highway 2, where the school bus takes him to school.

Gibby stomps on the accelerator. The bright green car zooms down the middle of the road. The guitars and words and drums scream from the Dart's speakers but seem to originate from the land around Gibby, from the soil itself. Gibby passes through the first gravel intersection, the road marker's pole catching the sun from its place in the ditch. Almost all of the street signs from Gibby's part of the county are currently stored under his bed. Once, when Gibby was very young, his father had told him that everyone should collect something, that it helped a person to understand the world. Gibby has gleaned little from the street signs though he looks at them nightly, hoping that one day soon he'll understand.

Now, Gibby thinks that he does understand. This trip is, has always been, his destiny. The signs are his parents, guiding Gibby from the grave. Gibby blinks and for a moment, past the windshield, it is snowing. The fields whip past, the car going faster, the music making the whole world breathe. Ahead, Gibby sees the highway. An enormous yellow tractor is blocking his path. Gibby swings the car to the left side of the road. Past the Terra-Gator, a sports car points toward him. 'Mustang,' Gibby breathes. He puts his hand down on the Dart's horn. He can't seem to bring his foot off the gas pedal. The Dodge takes to the air, crossing onto the blacktop. The last things Gibby remembers are a giant red eye and a wing.

*   *   *

The black-crowned night heron is badly off course. For three years, each June, the bird has come north from Mexico with its mate, migrating to Kansas to breed. This year, above Texas, smoke from grass fires filled the air, the two herons becoming separated from the flock. Over McAlester, Oklahoma, the pair had encountered hunters at dusk. The male waited by the body of its partner for a full day. It walked in circles, sounding its call, nudging the mate's corpse with its beak. When it understood that nothing would change, it kept going.

Climate shifts had forced the jet stream lower across the heartland, the strong winds pushing the heron east. North of Springfield, past the Ozarks, another day was lost to locating a food source – the brooks and small ponds had run dry or were gone; taking their place were paved lots and tall buildings. In a polluted marshland the heron ate three large creek chub, poisoning itself with mercury. By nightfall the bird had no feeling in one leg; when airborne the limb hung down uncontrollably.

The mercury had entered the brain of the heron above Iowa's southern border. It lost the ability to call out for help; feathers fell from the tips of its wings. Shaking too badly to stand still and hunt it took, instead, to scavenging, consuming what humans had killed in the course of their travels. The heron's eyes, bright red, glassed over with mucus. Its mind's fabric tore through completely. A night bird by nature, it flew during daylight, the bad limb still numb and dangling.

When it hits the car's windshield it passes no judgment. There is pain, and then there is nothing.

Gus Bender is in his backyard on his knees, applying mulch to Elizabeth's roses. With a bare hand he spreads the damp blend of wool scraps, sawdust, and grounds from his coffee, making a ring two inches from the base of each bush. Gus checks the Albas for mildew and aphids. With a spray bottle he mists every leaf.

It is Monday, just dawn, the Gator in the shop for the whole of the week. Soft light brushes the roses' white bulbs. To Gus's back are the long rows of soy crops, low and silent and green. The towing fees have taken the last of Gus's savings, money he'd meant for his trip to Atlanta, to check on his son. Gus has never been on an airplane; the concept is foreign, just short of frightful. With dew from the lawn soaking into his denims Gus thinks of himself seated, surrounded by strangers, their lives, for a short time, governed by one set of wings.

At the crash site, the two cars had collided head-on. Both drivers had been knocked unconscious. Gus had checked the green Dodge first, recognizing the vehicle as Agnes Swain's, a high-school classmate of Gus's parents. When he'd found the grandson, Gibby, slumped at the wheel, he'd been both relieved and angry.

The man in the sports car, whose name Gus has forgotten, was some sort of con man from one state east. He'd stumbled hysterically from his Mustang while Gus woke the teenager, unhurt and just short of weeping. Minutes earlier he had asked Gus for directions back up to I-80. After Gus had told him which roads to follow, he'd asked for a lift into town. The man had said no and walked back to his car. Gus told the investigating officers that it was around this time that he'd seen the green Dart approaching.

A semi with a flatbed dolly and tow winch had driven out from Council Bluffs, to transport the Gator. It had arrived well after all parties had left: the sheriffs, the motorist who had called the crash in, and the two victims in the back of an ambulance. While Gus had waited alone on the shoulder, he'd walked over to where the dead bird was. It lay flat on its stomach, its head spun around, its neck broken. From the impact half the bird's tail had been ripped from its body. Gus had searched the road for the clump of lost feathers, but they were nowhere to be seen.

Gus finishes with the mulch then sets down the bucket. He takes a pair of pruning shears from the tool loop on his jeans and thins out the center of each bush, removing the tips of the canes that have suffered from dieback. This year he's had problems with borers, sawfly and horntail, the larvae of both burrowing into the Albas' stems to feed. At the nursery in Treynor a woman had said to try Elmer's, a small dab of the glue at the point of each cane's trimming.

Gus has forgotten the glue in the mudroom. He rises, going to get it. As he does, pain coats his left arm and leg.

One side of his face loses feeling. Gus's blood seems to thicken then freeze in its veins. For a moment Gus is sure he is dying. He tries to prepare for this one final act. He is alone but does not want to be. The pain ebbs; soon, there is only a tingling. With his hand on his chest Gus walks toward the house. On the pan of his brain are base thoughts of survival: a glass from the cupboard, an aspirin from a bottle, the white stream of water from the tap on the sink. He stops to look out at the long rows of soy crops and considers the day he'll be buried near them, the land, once a floor, now a ceiling.

INDIVIDUALIZED
ALTIMETRY
OF STRIPES

Me and C.R., waiting on the five-year lag. Des Moines sucks. New development everywhere and people keep leaving. It's like making a broken boat bigger to stop the leak. Chicago or the coasts; anywhere but here, they go. At least Chicago's got a lake, a body of fucking water. It takes us three hours to get to the M-i-s-s-e-t-c, and that river looks like someone switched it off. No blue in the whole thing. That river's all wrong, I tell C.R., it's not even moving. C.R. says it is, it's just five years behind.

C.R. inks; I pierce. He did my sleeves and I put 16-gauge stainless on his tongue, four fat bearings the size of blueberries, except I did it crooked and they don't all quite line up. Told him I'd fix it when the healing was done, but C.R. says there's nothing to fix. I can do better, I tell him. You're doing fine, he says back. Wrists to shoulders I've got twin sunsets and elephants, black, in a ring around each forearm, connected trunk to tail. It was my idea but C.R. inked it in. I've got a red-winged blackbird at the base of my neck and my legs are done ankles to crotch; shamrocks around my areolas and eight balls on my thighs and question marks on the backs of my calves, pointing toward my feet. The only thing C.R. hasn't inked is my stomach. We're not sure what to put there yet. Next May we've been married five years; I met him at a bus stop, damn right, but you tell me a T-top Trans Am doesn't look good when you're taking the 46 from Connecticut Ave to New Mexico five times a week, to an apron at an Arby's. You tell me that isn't enough when you're fifteen and a good night at home is Stepdad Ray not sending his empty Lord Calvert bottle through the living-room window, and a bad night is keeping him out of your bed. You try those on for size and tell me which fits best.

A full moon, C.R. says, when we're naked on the futon, him drawing circles on my belly with a capped pen. A bowl of fruit. He's good with the needle but short on ideas; he did the heart on my fourth finger, small enough you can't see it under the ring. Over summer they started new development in the lot next to our apartment building but autumn got here early and the rigs bogged down in the mud. A lot of days now I feel lonely, and don't know why.

Me and C.R. both work at Great Planes but don't own it; Bob and Lucy, C.R.'s parents, do. They're fifty-five apiece. Lucy likes to say she was a slut back when it meant something. Bob asks her when that was. The lobby's filled with his drawings and there's a stack of three photo albums next to the register, with more. Lucy keeps shots of her work in a Hello Kitty purse under the counter, the pages of Polaroids of Labrets and Medusas, Orbitals and Madisons, and pierces below the belt, Apadravyas and Perineums and Fourchettes, rubber-banded together and dog-eared from age. The back room's surgery clean, the walls all white, and the twin dental chairs' red vinyl still smells new. This time of year we get college students most, boys from Creighton and Grinnell wanting a Celtic and asking if they can bring beer in. C.R. won't work on them since he got out of prison so Bob does. If they want piercings and try to flirt, I leave the gun down longer after the stud's gone through. Even the tough ones' eyes tear up after that, and if you think I wound up in this place because the world wasn't a little bit cruel to me, you're stupid, and if you think I'm not going to be a little bit cruel back, have a seat. We close every night at midnight, and we're open Christmas and New Year's Eve.

The day I met C.R. he'd just turned eighteen and gotten his first piece, the Hanged Man tarot card, on the palm of his hand. He stopped the Trans Am right in front of me and there wasn't an inch between the wheels and that curb. Whatcha up to, he said. I'm waiting at a bus stop, the fuck it look like, I said. My dad just gave me my first tattoo, said C.R. He held up a hand. Looks a lot like a bandage to me, I said. It's healing but that's temporary, C.R. replied, I got what's underneath for the rest of my life. Over the door inside Great Planes is a sign that says we're artists not tailors, and what we put on you we can't take off. Proceed at your own risk. You have any yourself, C.R. asked me. The cicadas were making their dumb, metal sounds and there was broken glass on the bus stop's bench. No one else was around and the sun was bright and hot. From inside the Trans Am, I could feel air conditioning. No, I said, I'm fifteen. Not for long, said C.R., but I got in the car when he leaned over and opened the door.

C.R. sees a doctor now. He got raped during his nineteen months in Anamosa Penitentiary. They had to put his intestines back in. He told me about it in a letter and all he wrote was they raped me and I had to get my intestines put back in. He got caught with dope at this bar, Shorty's, holding for a friend, and when the cops asked him to talk he'd stayed quiet, and got sent up. Our time together is different since, muted or more worn, and I wonder what work it might take for C.R. to fix himself. Last month the crown on the front of a water truck working on the lot next door to our apartment building got caught on the guy wire of a power line. It kept pulling and stretched the wire hard enough the overhead lines separated, and the hot wire fell on the derrick of the truck, and didn't ground out. The men working laid down running boards and jumped clear, and it took the fire department showing up and the engine's lights playing blue and red off the darkened walls of our apartment for C.R. to realize our power had gone out.

A mother wolf, he says, a tidal wave, an ocean. But none of those sound right to me.

Lucy says the five-year lag comes and goes, that sometimes the Midwest catches up to things before it falls behind again. Bob's inked the back of her legs to look like she's always wearing nylons, a single line that curves just right and runs from her thigh to her Achilles, cutting each leg in half. Just below her buttocks are tiny red bows, drawn to look pinned on even though they're permanent. I remember when T-shirts were a nickel for a pound, Lucy says to me, and the Goodwill left them in piles on the linoleum. You always have been picking your clothes up off of floors, says Bob. The two of them are beautiful, and immature, and will not have deciphered enough, I don't think, before they die. C.R. will not, either, but unlike his parents he has been damaged crucially, and most likely beyond repair, and this will make looking inside of himself painful always.

Shorty's closes at two, as is the standard in Iowa, and before C.R. got busted there the owner, Malky, would let us stay after hours and shoot nine-ball at the tables that weren't quarter slots. Great Planes sits mid-block, between a die-caster's and a glass factory, and we get everyone: the Harley guys; the metalheads; the Alpha Pi Omegas, who all want dolphins on their ankles. It got to be enough; I had C.R. ink the word DOLPHIN on my ankle and each autumn, when the blonde heiresses burst in, asking for them (my hair's red but dyed black), I pull down my sock and say, this, do you want it just like this? But it's not the word they're after it's the image and I can't stay mad at them for long because that's what I'm after, too, something that sums this all up without saying it outright. My body's almost covered. I'm running out of room.

Malky's full name is Malikai. He's a thin man with blue eyes, and his fine, brown hair is done in a bowl cut. The bar's called what it is from Malky's height, which, at five-one, is diminutive. He has no tattoos and nothing pierced and while Bob and Lucy have known him for decades, we went there mainly out of convenience, Shorty's being the only establishment nearby that was open. Malky's parents were cultists in Utah and he received, upon turning eighteen, a high sum from the Feds for this fact, a total that served the dual function of reparation and pay-off for remaining, in regard to the media, silent about how he grew up: the cult was housed in a defunct leather tanner's in a ghost town with no tourist appeal, and after agents negotiated the release of the children, the facility was burned, with the adults still inside it. In this manner Malky's youth was a series of sharp impacts and deleted scenes, and when he would tell us that he couldn't remember much about that time, we generally believed him, or at least understood that he couldn't yet say. The five-year lag comes and goes, and sometimes the Midwest catches up to things, before it falls behind again.

Once a week C.R. goes to a big glass building downtown and talks to a psychiatrist none of us has met. There, the man examines what has happened to C.R., and what is happening. My husband comes back to the shop quiet and with his eyes glassed over, and when we ask him how it went, he says it went good and sits in one of the back room's chairs and I think of Malky, behind the bar, washing the same dirty glasses over and over and over. I haven't seen Ray or my mom in seven years. You don't put the bad stuff behind you by talking about it for an hour every Wednesday.

On my back C.R.'s done an old-time pocket watch with gold chain, the lion from the Scottish flag, and a painting by Paul Klee – 'Individualized Altimetry of Stripes'. The first two are on either shoulder and the last takes up the rest of my back, starting over my lungs and ending at my kidneys. It would cost a customer two thousand dollars, or half of C.R.'s total bond.

Like Klee I have privatized my images, but found no universal truths. Around the question marks on my calves swim golden carp in black water. C.R. has drawn them to look fluid, moving, but they are going nowhere, swimming blind. When Bob leaves for a convention in Omaha or Peoria, Lucy fucks strangers in the back room's chairs. There is not a nicer way to say this because what is happening is not a nice thing. I want C.R. to look at my arms again, and to remind him, no, we'll never be able to forget what happened but the days go forward, anyway. But I don't know if the days are going forward for C.R.; I don't know if that's a universal truth. It's November now, and the bulldozer and single crane in the empty lot are wrapped in black, crinkly tarps. The lot's puddles of rainwater are brown as the Mighty Miss. The winds whip through the tarp's small tears and it sounds like they're popping and ripping apart. C.R. doesn't hear them. We sit on the futon naked, the television turned up. He and

Bob have a good relationship, better than most fathers and sons, but it is trade-based and bound only as tightly as shop talk will allow. Great Planes has a brass Sailor Jerry Bulldog, a handmade bronze Cuthook, a Brazilian Black Dragon with Benzmann grips. There is the horseshoe gun, too, the standby, its metal the same red as farmers paint their barns. The autoclave is a Ritter, an upright, and can clean ten needles at once. The lobby's walls are wood-paneled and the carpet the same red as the chairs in the back. I wanted a baby before C.R. went to prison, but now I wonder if I should leave him. Already the Trans Am's engine has been rebuilt and cold days the spark plugs don't take, and C.R. calls us a cab.

It's no vehicle for a child to ride in, I tell him.

You liked it just fine, he says back.

Bob has told me that for Christmas he is getting Lucy a dermal punch; instead of having to widen the hole in the ear lobe slowly, with bolts of increasing circumference, the dermal stamps the tissue right out.

On 35 north of Des Moines one needs to mind deer, even in the daytime. Farmers don't want them stealing feed so they leave small plates of honey laced with poison in the fields past their property lines. They use store-bought D-Con, which dehydrates and disorients. Days there's ditchwater near the highway's shoulder the deer drink and walk onto the blacktop, oblivious.

*　　*　　*

In Normal/Bloomington, there is a porn store that shares the same roof as a Pentecostal church. These two institutions are divided by a single granite wall and once a month, after Sunday sermon, the congregation fetches their picket signs from the broom closet behind the rows of pews and marches around to the other side of the building, singing hymns and declaiming their opinions. Sometimes paying customers emerge and unavoidably meet the group head on, embarrassed and adrenaline-licked as they walk with their heads down back to their cars.

Off I-80, just over the Nebraska border and into Wyoming, there is a sculpture of a coyote sitting on its haunches, mouth open and head pointed at the sky. The sculpture is ten feet tall and set at the top of a small bluff, next to the interstate. It will be on your left if you're going west. It won't be if you're not. Custom says it's good luck to leave something small on the sculpture's pedestal, something politely important: a shoelace, a money clip, a poem. When you pass the sculpture again, from the opposite direction, stop and see if the item is still there. If no, make a wish; you have helped someone. If yes, take it with you; it was meant to be yours forever.

At the shop, truckers come in and get new color put on old pieces. Their living is a lonely one but they sell the world well, and I think C.R. sometimes notices the intensity with which I listen to their stories. We married in a dun, blank field behind a Dairy Queen, the blue May sky that day filled with big gusts of wind, while we said our vows. In my most selfish moments, I am convinced they weren't enough; in my most cruel, I wish that what was done to C.R. in prison would have killed him. Instead we have become a long, slow thing, static and not worthless, but I am twenty-three, and don't want to start thinking about what could have been.

Lucy left home younger than I did, and with less. Des Moines makes it on every map, she says, Balko, Oklahoma, does not. Her home town is in that state's panhandle and I'm led to believe that if she hadn't hitched out to State 54 on the first day of eighth grade, and then much farther, and for decades, she would have had quite a different husband than Bob. I asked her once if Oklahoma is considered the Midwest, if it feels the five-year lag. She said Oklahoma is between Kansas and Texas, mainly, and that it feels nothing at all. I started apprenticing under her after C.R. went in for his bid, both to pass that time and because it was a certainty that I would learn what Lucy had to teach. Great Planes makes most of its money from inking, but Lucy is popular both for her beauty and expertise, and carries her own weight in currency. She says I have the hands and eyes for the work, and most importantly the patience. I worry I have fooled her on the last of these, have been diligent out of respect but not interest.

With the clocks switched back and Thanksgiving not far,

a necessary settling seems inevitable. The first snowfall will feel like soft electricity. Once my mother came to Great Planes, to get me to come back home. I was sixteen. Through the shop's small window I watched Ray's truck sit, idling, at the curb. C.R. has taken to watching the television into the morning hours, shows about Hun invasions and Viking landings, enhanced by computer effects re-enacting great battles, where flags fall and fake blood pools on shorelines, on cliffs. Our landlord is a large, creamy man whose bald head and small features give him the look of a boiled egg. His lust for me is obvious and sincere. I have wondered, more than once, how much sun the new building next door will block out from our windows. Behind this street's row of buildings is a bit of forest, a throwback to how the Midwest looked before it was harnessed and sewn. It seems impossible. Deer stand on its fringes. I knock on the window and they skitter away and I fill our plants' pots with water from a measuring cup. I have chosen species that need mild light and little precipitation. Even with a wet fall drought is a constant danger. Bob and Lucy say so many farmers have switched from corn to soy that you can see farther on the horizon now, that the Earth looks flatter than ever before. I do not disbelieve them. All I wanted from my mother's house fit in a single box, which C.R. carried from my old bedroom to the Trans Am while I waited in the passenger seat. I own no suitcase, and cannot remember the weight of one in my hand. The only other things I recall from the day my mom came to the shop are her voice saying my first name, and that one of her shoes had no shoelace.

Lucy lost her virginity when she was ten. Her hair is jet black and she dyes it that same color sometimes because she enjoys the process, the peroxide on her scalp, and the small tube of color like balm afterward. Bob is aware of her affairs and knows that they do not extend from spite, but rather as mandatory release. C.R. and I lived in the second bedroom of their home until I turned eighteen. For three hundred dollars a month they have five thousand square feet, the entire second floor of the warehouse that harbors the die-casting plant. At nine in the morning the dull reports of stamped metal sound from downstairs but it is a base noise, low and repetitive, and I have trained myself to ignore it. The fire escape descends to an alley, and Great Planes's back entrance; Bob and Lucy's commute is fifteen seconds, less if haste is needed. We open at ten in the morning, a time C.R. still finds early, and when he offers ideas for inking my stomach I remind him what a baby will mean. Since his release, now almost a year behind him, his plans for our future have streamlined. In earlier times he had promised our own shop, or no shop, a clean break and move to a new place, but these cities and smaller, coastal towns never gained names and more than once C.R. has talked of the time that Bob and Lucy will be too old to remain perfect at what they do, and that Great Planes can be ours. He's put this moment as close as five years away. His thin frame gained weight in prison until he got raped, and couldn't eat. He has Lucy's hair, jet black and with a hint of curl to it, and he goes long stretches now without blinking his blue eyes, so long that they must go out of focus. Around C.R.'s right arm, from wrist to shoulder, is inked a rough map of the Midwest: the Dakotas to Lake Michigan, Nebraska to the Illinois/Indiana border. Our plan was to get each state done a different color but only after we'd spent a night in it together; we'd see these composites, sometimes, on the sides of RVs. Up my husband's left leg runs the Pacific seaboard; up the right, the Atlantic. The only state that's been colored in is Iowa. I would like a baby. That its blankets would grow softer with each washing, that it would have favorite toys each month, each day, each week. At the Hy-Vee, C.R. buys diet cola and microwave popcorn in bulk. His left arm is still blank entirely. No sun has left its skin the color of lint.

The boy C.R. was holding for is named Dudley; he lives in Florida now, in Orlando. Recently he has taken to sending postcards to C.R., asking for money from him. On the front of the latest was the Epcot Center, its dome against a deep blue sky. The back read:

CAMERON RICHARD – TOUGH TIMES ARE A DIME A DOZEN, AND I'M DOWN TO SHITTING NICKELS. I THOUGHT I HAD A JOB WORKING OVERNIGHTS AT A FUNERAL HOME, BUT THEY GAVE IT TO SOMEONE ELSE. A MAN I MET RENTS

A P.O. BOX; YOU COULD SEND THE MONEY THERE. ANYTHING HELPS. I HATE FLORIDA. I THINK I KNOW WHAT YOU WENT THROUGH NOW, IN PRISON. – D

I've forgiven Dudley as much as I'm going to, and his life will be a hard one for he has little to offer anybody, and does not make friends with ease. There have been over a dozen postcards in total, which leads me to believe that C.R. is sending him money in secret. I take this action as just short of deceitful, just short of a reason to leave. Dudley wished for C.R.'s talent with the needle but had none, nor could he ever save money for more than small impersonal pieces chosen from the walls of Great Planes's lobby and inked on by C.R. after business hours, for free. I put a knife through Dudley's hand the last time I saw him, when he came in the shop's door after C.R. had been sent to prison. I don't know what his intentions were, but when he put his palms down on the countertop's wood, I took the bowie we keep under the register for emergencies and pinned his left hand where it lay. Dudley screamed like a child when the metal went through, piercing all of it: skin, tendon, bone. We're calling the cops, Lucy said over his howling. Damn right you're calling the cops, Dudley said back, and pointed a finger on his free hand at me. Let her go be with her man if she wants to so badly. We'll say you tried to rob us, Lucy told him, holding the phone's receiver in the air. I'm dialing right now.

Behind her, Bob stood with his arms crossed over his stomach; on each biceps he has a red, full heart inked on the hill of the muscle, and with his teeth set he flexed one arm then the other, the hearts taking turns beating. Pull it out, Dudley pleaded. Already the swelling had made the hand turn lightly purple. Pull it out, and it's like nothing happened, he swore to me.

Often now C.R. is gone for longer than the hour and a half it takes him to drive to the big glass building, sit in an expensive room, and drive back. When I asked him where he goes he told me that he buys lunch at a fast-food restaurant across the street, and sits there and eats it alone. Some nights the tarps crack like thunder and I jump in C.R.'s arms. In better times he would have made fun of my skittishness; now he only asks what's wrong. I took a cab once, downtown, to see if C.R.'s story was true. It was. From across the street, at a bus stop, I watched him through the restaurant's window. He sat hunched in his chair, staring at the plastic table like a book or magazine was right there, open in front of him. From their carton on a brown tray, C.R. took a single French fry at a time, without looking. Each golden strip lasted three separate bites. At one point C.R. stopped and set the fry, partially consumed, back in its carton. After that, he folded his hands in his lap and stared straight ahead, at nothing.

I did what Dudley asked me to, but not before moving the blade around in the wound and making it bigger, making it something that he would remember for the rest of his life.

On rare occasions collectors come to Great Planes; they schedule appointments weeks and months ahead of time, often calling from out of state or other continents, from California or Berlin or Japan. Bob runs his business on work ethic and pleasant ways, and in this manner the Midwest suits him. He has thick glasses with black, unfashionable frames, and his ponytail is graying, and halfway down his back. He wears Hawaiian shirts and navy-blue work pants and says he was wearing the same thing twenty-five years ago, when Great Planes's first customer, a collector named David – who is in the shop today, right now – came through the door with a print of the painting by the Regionalist Grant Wood, a copy of his famous work, *American Gothic*. Most people have seen it, even if they don't know it by name; it's the portrait of the farmer holding a pitchfork, his wife standing next him, looking off into the distance. The piece is expensive and quite time-consuming, but David is wealthy, having made his money in hydraulics, in the practical applications of liquid in motion, and Bob has come to view its completion as the biggest test of his skill. To get the correct shade of red he blends Chinese inks with Aboriginals, special-ordering from Beijing, Sydney, beyond. Every year David returns and has work added; the painting runs from his neck to the base of his tailbone, and over all the skin between.

I would like a baby, and there is the shop to get lost in: the cardboard boxes of barbells and CBRs; the small packets of Provon and Satin and A&C, used for protection on a new piece; the hundreds and hundreds of sketches. Lucy has started me reading manuals on piercing with the circulatory system in mind, thick guides on how to put a needle through anything and avoid hitting a nerve. David's back is two-thirds done but there are still items missing, and whole areas not even begun. Though getting older, David has kept himself in shape, and only now are the smallest pockets of fat starting to sit on his hips, the muscle too tired to remain muscle. The Wood piece is not his only one but the rest of his work is below the belt, done from waist to feet, tribal pieces collected from artists in the Philippines, Chile, the Ivory Coast. David takes his shirt off and to look at him from the front, one would think a needle has never touched his skin. I cannot say the same of myself, and do not know what will happen to me. Bob puts the dentist's chair horizontal and David lies on it, stomach pressed to the vinyl. The ink gun's switch is flipped, and the needle starts to buzz so fast it doesn't look like it's moving at all. David turns in the chair and holds a hand up, gesturing for Bob to wait. C.R. and Lucy and me are gathered around the two of them. *Whoa, whoa, whoa*, David says, *hold on a second*. This is an old joke, one that we all know. The ink gun is humming. C.R. puts his hand over mine. *Now before we start I have to ask – are you sure you know what you're doing?*

RUMSPRINGA

Coy woke naked on the bare floor of Teshram's trailer. Outside, summer had come to an end. The weekend was to bring the first of the autumn freezes. The cold would turn the trees. Coy coughed and rolled onto his side, blinking. There were goose bumps over the backs of his arms. He looked around the trailer for his clothes and couldn't find them. Sunday was Coy's twenty-first birthday. He thought about iced roads and wrecked crops.

On the far side of the room, near the trailer's kitchenette, two boys sat in front of a muted television. The appliance was perched on one corner of a large cardboard box, its sides creased and failing. The taller of the boys was holding a controller attached to Teshram's game machine. On the TV's screen, a rifle sight lined up the top of a man's head. In the next second the man's head exploded and the body fell to the ground, and was gone.

Coy grabbed the blue wool blanket hanging over the arm of the plaid sofa. He wasn't sure if he'd gone to sleep on the piece of furniture or the floor. He stood up, wrapping the blanket around his midsection. Overnight his needle had fallen into the full ashtray on the side table, its tip sunk in the tan clump of butts. Beer bottles stood upright and turned over on the doublewide's linoleum, in groups of threes and fours. Coy's whole body ached. His wrists felt hollow and his hands were trembling. There was a bad taste in his mouth. He was out of heroin. He needed more.

The door to the trailer's single bedroom was shut. Coy walked over to it, moving through the morning light let in by the window's blinds. Outside he heard the familiar clopping of a shoed horse and the turn of buggy wheels over gravel. Next to the ashtray the cordless phone was missing from its port.

Something happened on the television and one of the boys exclaimed quietly. Coy turned to look at them, his blond hair falling in his eyes. They were sixteen most likely, just starting their rumspringa. Both were in shorts and white church shirts and sat cross-legged, a sandwich bag of marijuana between them on the floor.

'Do you know if Teshram's sleeping?' Coy asked.

'I heard the toilet running a little bit before,' the boy holding the controller said, not taking his eyes off the screen.

Coy adjusted the blanket and with his free hand knocked on the door. It was made of ply balsa and top-hinged only and when Coy knocked the door swung, moving away from him and back again, banging against the frame.

'Teshram, are you awake?' Coy asked.

'I guess so,' he heard Teshram say.

Coy managed the door open. His cousin was lying in bed, legs crossed under a flat gray flannel sheet. The stacked pair of king-size mattresses took up most of the room's floor space. In one corner stood a short desk, its front legs lengths of rebar. White sheets of thin cotton hung over each of the room's three windows, their edges yellowing and curled.

Teshram was a head taller than Coy and five years older; over Labor Day weekend he'd turned twenty-six. He had a long face with ponds of freckles on his cheeks and the same light blond hair as Coy had. Across his chest was a tattoo, three words: EAT FUCK KILL, done in black ink and outlined in red. The dot on the KILL's 'I' was a burn from a pot pipe, its metal bowl heated and pressed to the skin, leaving a scar in the shape of a perfectly round circle. The interior of the circle held the same black as the tattoo's lettering. Coy knew how Teshram had gotten the burn because Coy was the person who had given it to him.

'Have you seen my clothes?' Coy asked.

'You set them on fire. They're gone now.'

'When?'

'Last night in the yard.'

'Why'd I do that?'

'You don't remember? It's not that far back to think.'

Coy tried to put the days in order. He remembered fixing in the bathroom of the Dairy Queen some recent afternoon, maybe yesterday, then ordering a pineapple milkshake and sitting with it outside on the shop's curb, in the sun. The milkshake had been too thick to suck through the straw and Coy had forgotten to get a spoon from the self-serve counter. He hadn't wanted to go back inside so he'd tossed the whole thing in the trash.

'Did we go into town yesterday?' Coy asked. 'To the Dairy Queen?'

Teshram nodded, pushing himself up with an elbow. From the floor next to him he grabbed his lighter and cigarettes. 'Yeah, man. But we went there the day before, too.'

'I really need a fix, Teshram. It's sorta bad.'

'It's ten in the morning, Coy. You should start being careful about that.'

'Yeah, I know, I will be. But do you have anything? I could use it. I'll pay you back soon, I swear.'

When Teshram turned eighteen and didn't rejoin the church, he'd enlisted and drawn assignment to an Army base in Germany. For two weeks he did oil changes on supply trucks in a vehicle bay. He was walking back to his barracks after sundown when he'd been hit from behind by an officer driving a Jeep. Teshram's left ankle had shattered, the bigger bone breaking, both tendons detaching from the bone. After surgery the Army gave him an honorable discharge and a set of crutches and sent him back home to Indiana. Coy had gone to meet him at the bus station in Terre Haute. It was the only time he'd ever left the county.

Teshram set a green glass ashtray on his chest, over the middle word in his tattoo.

'I'll give you some, Coy, but you have to do a favor for me. You have to go down and get Marcy out of jail. Her bond's three hundred dollars. The money's in the drawer in my desk.'

'Okay, Tesh. I'll be back in a half-hour.'

'No,' Teshram said, 'you won't. She's not in jail here. That's the thing.'

'Where's she in jail?'

'In Kentucky.'

'Near Stateline?'

Teshram shook his head. 'No, she's way down 64. Close to West Virginia. She used to live over there, I guess.'

Teshram smeared the end of his cigarette on the ashtray's bottom. The ember fell off and continued to smoke. Coy thought about roads he didn't know and the sheriffs along them, hiding on turn-offs Coy couldn't see. His legs felt weak, either from the drugs he needed or from what Teshram was asking of him.

'Can't you do it, Tesh? I don't feel good. I need to brush my teeth.'

'Brush your teeth and take a shower,' said Teshram. 'What you need to feel better is in the drawer with Marcy's bond. Are those kids still here?'

Coy nodded. 'Where'd they come from?'

'North Texas,' said Teshram. 'Their friends left three days ago after the field party and forgot them and last night they wound up here.'

Coy stood in the doorway, not saying anything.

'I'd get Marcy myself, Coy, but there's people coming over. I need to be at the house. Make sure those kids go out for a few hours. And take extra money for gas for the car.' Teshram rolled onto his side and pulled the sheet over the top of his head, revealing his feet. Coy stared at the long scar running up the side of his ankle, a single line with small dots on either side of it, like the middle line and reflectors on a blacktop.

'Do you have *any* money, Coy? I bet you don't. I bet if I could see you, you'd be shaking your head.'

'Why'd I burn my clothes, Teshram?' Coy asked.

'Because you didn't want them anymore,' Teshram said.

Half an hour later Coy slid the seat up in Teshram's dark blue Ford Torino. He ran a hand through his still-damp hair. On the kitchenette's counter he'd done two large rails of heroin, one with each nostril, and had enough for two more wrapped in tinfoil in the elastic band of his borrowed underpants. He felt better but not good, the way a person feels the day after a flu. Coy could see the boys from earlier, the Texans, walking down the road into town. Their footsteps brought up dust from the gravel. Some yards from the

Torino was a small pile of black soot, the remains of Coy's clothes. A button from his church shirt hadn't melted; it sat on the edge of the ash, catching light from the sun. Coy turned the engine over and let it idle, the alternator bouncing the rpms before leveling out.

Coy took the car toward the highway's entrance, away from town. He passed the dirt turn-off to where the field party had happened three nights ago. In the grass ditch was a red balloon, its rubber puckered but still holding air. Coy, like his cousin, had forsworn the church following his rumspringa. None in their community would speak to either of them ever again. Since his decision over a year ago Coy had seen his parents only once, passing their buggy while riding in the front seat of Teshram's automobile. He hadn't waved and they hadn't waved back. All of Coy's things were still at their house, in his old bedroom. From its perch on a field post, a crow watched Coy pass in the Torino. It waited for the dust to settle, then flew across the road.

Coy drove south on US 41, the Illinois/Indiana border out the window to his right. A railroad matched the highway's path, two lines over the flat green farmland. North of Evansville Coy turned east, onto Interstate 64. He crossed into Kentucky at Louisville, almost hitting a truck pulling horses when he tried to get out of an exit lane. In a short while the landscape around him filled up with hills and Coy got anxious. The sky seemed to have shrunk. Marcy was two hours away, in a jail cell in a town called Loess. Teshram's jeans were too long and Coy had to cuff them over. The rolled denim was wide at his ankles and kept catching the corner of the Torino's brake pedal. At an exit before Frankfort Coy pulled off the highway for gas.

Inside the food mart Coy bought a root beer and a pouch of beef jerky. Both were brands he'd never seen before. The unfamiliar names and packaging excited him. He remembered the first time he'd entered a grocery store, the week after he'd turned sixteen. Most of the township took their children on shopping trips but Coy's parents forbade it, saying he could wait until rumspringa and see it on his own. When Coy had first stepped through the grocery's sliding door he'd started laughing. There were so many new things it seemed impossible. He'd wanted all of them, right then.

Coy paid for his meal and gasoline, asking the attendant for the lavatory's key. He walked to the back of the store and opened the bathroom door and locked it again behind him. From his waistband he took out the bindle of tinfoil, unfolding it on top of the hand dryer mounted to the wall. Coy arranged two thin lines of heroin using the edge of his driver's license, saving half of what Teshram had given him for the trip home. He hoped that Marcy would offer to drive back to Indiana but couldn't count on it, so he rationed – he wouldn't be able to manage the car if he had nothing at all.

In the chrome dryer's reflection, Coy watched himself roll up a dollar bill.

The Torino drove well and there was still heat in Kentucky, the day warm. Coy passed the exits for Frankfort, then Lexington. The hills spread out on either side of the highway and grew taller and tree-covered. Coy lost the radio station he'd been listening to. The interstate was raised above the floor of the valley by a good twenty feet, and every so often Coy would notice roads running perpendicular to the highway. He passed a truss bridge with a CLOSED sign hanging from its lead beam. Further on he passed a church, its white spire peeking up past the route's guard rail. Coy saw the marker for Montgomery County and began looking for the next exit. According to Teshram, Marcy was not far up one of these roads.

The off-ramp Coy needed came five minutes later. He signaled and descended its slope, stopping Teshram's car at the base of the hill. Coy stretched his fingers, the butts of his palms pressed against the steering wheel. It was just past four in the afternoon. The interstate, to Coy's left, cast a thick shadow on the asphalt between the intersection and overpass. Out of the darkness a police cruiser appeared. Coy sat up, his fingers curling. He hadn't been wearing his seat belt since the gas station. Coy felt the tinfoil press against his skin. The cruiser slowed, crossing in front of the Torino. Coy watched it pass. LOESS POLICE was written in gold letters on the rear of the vehicle, one word on either side of the trunk's keyhole. The brown car continued past Coy, accelerating as it climbed the road's hill.

Coy sat there, white-knuckled. After some moments he clicked in his three-point, then rolled down his window and spat. A flatbed semi hauling a backhoe had come down the off-ramp behind him. It blasted its horn at the Torino, waiting to move. The cruiser had gone in the direction Coy needed to go, too. He turned right, forgetting to signal, and followed it.

At the hill's crest a square green sign with white letters spelled out LOESS. Below the single word was the number fifty-six. The town sat plumb in a small, tight valley, surrounded by forest on all sides. Coy followed the hill's steep drop, the cruiser still ahead of him. The road reached town and leveled out. Coy passed a defunct hardware store and working barbershop and a Pentecostal church. Houses sat back from the road in places, their vinyl siding streaked with rust. Around some of the homes' dirt yards ran wire fences. The cruiser was the only car on the street.

The police station was at the far end of town, the road beyond curving sharply and disappearing past a bank of limestone. The cruiser pulled in to the building's lot, next to an old-model Bronco. The only space open was alongside the cruiser's left. Coy rolled the Torino in slowly then shut the engine off. He opened the car's door and stood up.

The sheriff who got out of the cruiser was thinner than Coy. Below his gun belt his tan trousers bunched. He had a brown mustache and wore sunglasses and a full-brimmed patrol hat. The man walked to the front of the Torino, looking Coy in the face.

'Help you?' the man said, stopping in front of the Torino's left headlight. His accent was thick and he spoke quickly, and it took Coy a moment to figure out what he had said.

'I'm looking for Marcy Haysi,' Coy told him. 'I've got her bond.'

'All right,' the sheriff told him. 'Come on and we'll get you two set up.' Coy locked the car and walked past the man, to the building's wood front door. He'd meant to put the tinfoil in the glove compartment but there'd been no chance to do it. He was terrified. He wondered if dogs could smell drugs through tinfoil. He wondered if these cops had dogs.

The inside of the station was a single room, poorly lit and smelling of sulfur. The walls were wood-paneled and the ceiling light was a single exposed bulb. A small window faced toward the street. Next to it a second sheriff sat behind a metal desk, a table lamp illuminating the keys of his typewriter. The man glanced up when Coy opened the door. Upon seeing the other sheriff he looked down again. Ahead of Coy was a short hallway lined with twin rows of steel bars. Between two of the bars, perched on a cross beam, were a woman's hands.

'This man's here to pick up Marcy,' the first sheriff said, closing the door behind him. 'He's driving on Indiana tags.'

'I got friends in low places,' said the second sheriff. 'That was on the radio today, that song.' Reluctantly he pressed both index fingers to the typewriter's keys. Four of the machine's teeth sprung up at once. Under his breath the sheriff cussed.

'I'm going to put this thing through my wood chipper, I swear it. I'm not cut out for this, John.' He was older than the first sheriff and overweight, clean-shaven and with gray hair.

'Get Miss Haysi's paperwork, Curtin. I'll worry on the report.'

The older sheriff took a deep breath and pushed himself up from the desk. He walked to a row of black file cabinets behind him and opened one.

'This'll take a second,' the younger sheriff told Coy. 'You can go back and see her if you want.'

Coy nodded. The small bit of heroin in his system had begun to work itself out again. He took a first step and almost collapsed. The younger sheriff looked at him. Coy's head felt light and his body heavy. When the drug ran its course these feelings would reverse, and Coy would need more.

John replaced Curtin in front of the typewriter, taking out the piece of paper and putting in a different, smaller one. Coy walked back to the jail. Inside the cell was Marcy. She was smiling and had on a white T-shirt under denim coveralls, her black hair over their straps. She looked at Coy with her bright blue eyes. When she saw it was him that had come to get her, not Teshram, she stopped smiling and looked at the floor.

'Hi, Marcy,' Coy said.

'Hey, Coy.'

'You ready to go back to Indiana?'

'I guess I am. Where's your cousin?'

'He's at home. He had some people coming over.'

Marcy nodded. She had been living off and on at Teshram's since winter. Last May she turned forty. Marcy worked at the gas station that was walking distance from the trailer. She would quit and leave town and the owner would rehire her when she returned. Teshram told Coy that she'd always keep coming back because Teshram never made her pay for her drugs.

'You make a wish before going into Eastern Time?' Marcy asked, looking up at Coy.

'What?' Coy said.

'At Louisville you switch over to Eastern Time. You're an hour older than you would be on normal. You're supposed to make a wish.'

The inside of the cell was painted gunmetal. Bolted to its back wall was a steel-framed cot. A small sink stood in one corner and there was no toilet. Coy wondered what Marcy did when she had to go the bathroom. He needed to go himself.

'I didn't make a wish,' Coy told her. He could hear the sheriff typing. 'I didn't know I was supposed to do that.'

'Why don't you go pay that bond, Coy? I can drive the way back if you want. Did you bring the Torino?'

Coy nodded.

'I love that car,' said Marcy. She smiled like she was turned on. The skin around her eyes wrinkled up.

Coy walked back to where the sheriffs were. He didn't know where to stand so he stood in the middle of the room, below the light. He was sweating badly and it was making the tinfoil move from its spot in his waistband. Coy was sure it would fall down his pants leg and onto the floor. The older man, Curtin, was still bent over the file cabinet. The younger sheriff stopped typing and looked up.

'We're gonna need your driver's license,' he told Coy. 'The total on the bill comes to three hundred and seventy-four.'

'How much?' Coy asked.

The sheriff looked at the piece of paper in the typewriter. He said the same number again.

'I don't have that much,' Coy said.

'Then why'd you come all the way down here?' asked the sheriff.

'My cousin told me to,' said Coy. 'He said the bond was three hundred exactly.'

'It is,' the sheriff said, 'but that doesn't include the ticket I'm typing out for you not signaling at the intersection. I could write you on a belt violation, but this ticket's cheaper. It's whichever you want.'

From Teshram's jeans pocket Coy pulled out all the money

he had. His cousin had given him four hundred in twenties, one hundred in gas money and three more for the bond. Coy counted the bills out then studied the coins. He was four dollars and forty cents short.

'I have three-seventy,' he told the sheriff, rounding up.

'That car out there belong to you?'

'It belongs to family,' said Coy.

'You're not registered on it?'

'No.'

'Uh-oh,' said Curtin. He shut the file cabinet's door and turned around.

'How old are you, son?' the younger sheriff, John, asked him.

'I'm nineteen,' said Coy.

'See,' John said, 'now what I'll say isn't meant to insult you, but you've hit on an awkward age. By law you aren't a kid anymore and by looks you aren't an adult. Four dollars may not seem like much but we accept four short on every ticket we give and we'd bankrupt the county.'

'They'd hang us,' said Curtin. He put his hands around his neck like he was choking himself then started laughing. His face went red.

The younger man smiled and rubbed one side of his mustache. 'And you got a car that you don't own out there and laws you've broken with it, and fines that you cannot pay. Your name's Coy, right? That's what I heard Miss Haysi say?'

'Yes, sir,' Coy said.

'What's your last name, Coy?'

'Yoder.'

'What's going on out there?' Marcy called. 'Coy?'

Both men ignored her. John went on talking. He still had his sunglasses on. 'So what I can do, Mr Yoder, is either treat you like a kid, and let you pay what money you have and take Marcy out of here, or go on and treat you like an adult. And in truth I'm not sure which seems proper to me. I'm not sure of which thing to do.'

Coy didn't say anything. He thought that he was going to faint standing up. The light swam over the brown walls of the room. Both of the sheriffs were staring at him. It seemed to Coy he'd arrived here out of error, that the events that were currently happening to him couldn't actually be happening.

'I need to use your bathroom,' Coy said. 'Can I?'

'You can,' the younger sheriff told him. 'It's around the side of the building, to the right.'

'Okay,' said Coy. He walked to the station door and opened it and closed it again behind him. Coy looked back in the direction of the road he'd come in on. No light shone from any of the houses. The sun had begun to move behind the hills and the trees' shadows were fuller now, the forest more dense.

The bathroom was almost identical to the one at the gas station, white-tiled with a single stall and sink. Coy took out the tinfoil and wiped the moisture from it, holding it in his fist while he used the toilet. He thought about keeping the bindle in his shoe but worried that it would make him walk funny and the sheriffs would notice. Coy set it back in his waistband, over the bone of his hip, deciding he would put it in the Torino before he went back inside. He wanted very badly to be on the plaid sofa in Teshram's trailer, with a spoon and lighter and syringe. For Coy, his rumspringa had not lasted long enough. All the field parties and drugs and driving fast in cars were done with the understanding that they were temporary pleasures, and that access to them would cease when he returned to the church. Coy hadn't wanted them to end. Teshram's trailer was only two miles from the township but it was a world away. In his first week of staying there Coy had eaten his first pizza and drunk his first beer. He'd smoked marijuana from a bong and speed from a glass pipe in the shape of a daisy. In the back seat of Teshram's car he'd kissed a girl and she'd let him put his hand down her pants. Coy couldn't imagine returning to a life without these things in it. They were better than anything he'd known before and always would be. They belonged to him.

Coy considered removing the dope and doing all of it on the back of the stall's toilet. He could flush the tinfoil, leave the Torino, and get back to the highway on foot. Teshram had once hitched all the way to Chicago with a trucker, and truckers would know where drugs could be bought.

Next to the sink's faucet was a small plastic bottle of hand soap. Coy pressed some out and turned the faucet on, washing his hands. The soap's scent matched that of the shampoo his parents used to buy at the supermarket, bright and floral and fresh. Coy remembered his small room on the second story of their home, his single bed and set of three windows that looked east. His father worked at the furniture store owned by the township, and one summer he and Coy had built a bird bath of white oak, with a stone bath for the water to sit in. They had put the bath in the part of the yard below Coy's bedroom windows. It occurred to Coy now that he would never see it again.

When Coy opened the door to the bathroom John was standing outside, waiting for him. He'd taken off his sunglasses and Coy could see his eyes. They were long and oval-shaped, and their color was a strange green closer to yellow. 'I figured out what we're gonna do,' the sheriff told Coy. He was holding his gun in his hand.

He motioned for Coy to walk around to the front of the building. Coy did. Resting against the grille of the parked Bronco was Curtin. Steam rose from a cup of coffee he was holding. Behind him, on the truck's hood, was a shotgun, its barrel pointed toward a patch of woods on the building's far side.

'Do you know what Marcy did to get in here?' John asked. Coy shook his head.

'She killed her ex-husband's dog,' said Curtin. 'Cooked it.' He smiled at Coy then blew on his coffee but didn't take a sip.

'Why'd she do that?' Coy asked. He didn't know that Marcy had been married, or divorced.

'Somewhere amongst Marcy's relatives there's coal money,' John said. 'She's a ways off from the trunk of the family tree, but it's there. You wouldn't know it on looking at her but she's a smart one, too. She grew up in Huntington and did three years on a four-year degree.'

'Anthropology,' said Curtin. 'Ancient cultures and what not.'

'You go to college?' John asked Coy.

Coy shook his head. He thought sometimes that he wanted to.

'Well Marcy was studying up,' John said. 'But on weekends her folks made her come over to Kentucky and help out the relatives, so she'd be earning the inheritance she had coming down the road. She'd cut paychecks or file papers, something easy. After a while, though, Marcy got bored.'

The sheriff ejected the clip from his weapon, popping out the bullets with his thumbnail. Coy watched them jump into the sheriff's palm. When he had the clip emptied, he put the bullets in his trouser pocket and the clip back in the gun.

'Not a lot of women work coal, so if one's at the plant and wants attention, she can get some. Marcy got hers from

Hank Locke. He drove a truck bringing payload in from the auger mines. And he and Marcy, they thought they might be in love. Only the rest of Marcy's family didn't think so, and to get things bad between them they laid Hank off. He and Marcy came down here so Hank could work timber and a month later they tied the knot. You see the hardware shop coming in?'

Coy nodded.

'They lived right behind there. Marcy didn't want kids so Hank bought her a dog, this small thing, a lapdog is what they call it, I guess, though I couldn't know the breed.'

'A Pekinese,' said Curtin. 'Hank bought Marcy a Pekinese.'

'Yeah, a Pekinese,' said John. 'Marcy had the same kind growing up, and it made her happy, having something from her youth around her. Anyway a barn rat could have given orders to this thing. It weighed maybe eight pounds. And Marcy loved it first off. But she didn't love Hank's new job. He clear-cut and the crew he worked on was back in the forest, in deep timber, for weeks straight.'

'She felt slighted,' said Curtin. 'Her word.'

John nodded his head. 'And she'd read a book back in Huntington that said the ancient Greeks had this torture device that was a metal bull. The bull was hollow inside and the Greeks put folks they captured in it, then lit a fire underneath. The heat sucked all the oxygen out. Whoever was in there suffocated while they cooked to death. Marcy did that same thing with the dog. Only she didn't use a metal bull. She just taped the lid shut on a corn pot and turned on the stove.'

'It was a nice wedding, though,' said Curtin.

'You were there?' asked Coy.

'Sure he was,' John said. 'We both were. Hank Locke was this man's son.'

Curtin raised his eyebrows at Coy then drank from his coffee. The town's valley was losing its light.

'I mention it because sometimes things get killed on accident and sometimes things get killed on purpose. To square your debt you're gonna try at the second of these things right now.'

'Are you much of a marksman?' Curtin asked.

'No,' said Coy.

'Then this might be a little tough,' said John.

Curtin lifted up the shotgun from the Bronco's hood and started walking toward the forest. John told Coy to follow the other sheriff then fell in step behind, leaving the building's lot for a deer path that snaked back into the trees. Coy wondered if the sheriffs were going to shoot him and make it look like Coy had tried to shoot them. For a moment this thought was calming to Coy. Tiny metallic explosions swam across his vision when he blinked. Coy put his head down between his legs and threw up. Tears pooled at the corners of his eyes. He spat and wiped at his mouth with the back of his hand. Both the sheriffs stopped walking and considered him.

'You going to be all right?' Curtin asked.

Coy nodded. 'Just tell me what I have to do so I can leave,' he said.

'We'll do better than that,' said John.

The three of them went deeper into the woods, John leading now and Curtin behind Coy. Brown nettles covered the forest's floor. The air smelled thickly of pine. The path wound away from the station, away from the road and the homes. Coy heard a truck pass, downshifting. After some minutes of walking in silence, John stopped.

Coy reached the sheriff and looked past him. Trees ringed a clearing in the forest; amongst their branches were dozens of wooden bird houses, hanging from strings. In the middle of the clearing was a long granite bench. On its seat and in the branches of the trees and amongst the clearing's stumps and junegrass were birds, more than Coy could count. He saw blue jays and cardinals and other smaller types, finches or sparrows, with brown heads and tan wings. He saw a pair of robins frozen at the clearing's far edge. From its perch on a feeder box Coy watched a rock dove lift flapping to the air and land again in the very same spot.

'Before my son died,' Curtin said, 'he built this place for me. Got the trees out and bought the granite from a quarry a county up. He ran a sander out here on an extension cord and buffed down the edges of the bench. Built the bird houses, too. He said it would be a nice place to come and sit.'

Curtin walked past Coy, to the clearing's fringe. Some of the birds on the bench and grass scattered, taking to the limbs of the trees.

'On the other side of the interstate back there,' said Curtin, 'there was a rail bridge. It was an old thing that people knew they weren't supposed to use but did anyway. My son, Hank, got home from the forest and found the dog he'd given Marcy in the pot.'

'She'd put a bow on the top of it and left town,' John said. 'Like Santa Claus.'

Curtin nodded. 'On the far side of the bridge is a cemetery where folks would take their pets. Most people around here hunt and when a dog goes some get impractical and want to bury it. Hank wanted to do the same for the Pekinese, so he drove it out there. The bridge had a length of chain link at either end, so you had to get out of your car twice, once before you got on the bridge and a second time, after you already were.'

The sheriff took a sip of his coffee then dumped the rest out onto the forest floor. 'There'd been good snow last winter and the bridge was heavy from it. Hank was taking the chain off the bridge's far side when the wood gave under the weight of his truck. You can tell a kid the same thing six different ways, six hundred times. They're going to listen firstly how they listen last, which is not at all.

I told Hank to stay off that truss since he could walk. And that was back when they still ran rail on it. The river is twenty feet down. Hank's truck landed on top of him. My wife died five years ago, in a hospital in a town she'd never been to before. Hank was our only child.'

Curtin crumpled up the styrofoam cup. It made an awful noise and Coy thought he might be sick again. John put the empty pistol to Coy's chest.

'Pick your bird,' John said, holding out a bullet. 'You get one shot. You kill something we let you out of here with Marcy and you get to you keep your money. You miss, though, and you still owe us on both.'

Coy took the gun from the sheriff. The weapon felt impossibly heavy; it pulled on Coy's shoulder and wrist. The raised grains of its handle were cold and hard.

'You know how to load that thing?' asked Curtin.

Coy shook his head. He had never held a gun before.

The older sheriff leaned his shotgun against a pine tree and took the pistol and loaded it, then handed it back to Coy.

'Why do you want me to shoot at these birds?'

'Because if I can't come back here,' Curtin told Coy, 'I don't want anything to.'

Coy could barely feel his hands. He scanned the clearing, sweeping the pistol out at the birds. John and Curtin stepped back behind him. The forest glowed bruised in the dusk.

Coy brought the gun up close to his face. He closed his

right eye and sighted, the way he'd seen actors do on cop shows on TV. The scent of the bathroom soap still clung to him. Coy settled on one of the plump robins frozen on the clearing's far side.

'Move your legs out wider,' said Curtin.

'It's going to kick,' said John. 'It's going to fight you more than you think it would.'

Coy took a deep breath, spread his feet, and shot. The blast annihilated the quiet. The recoil forced Coy's arms over his head. Bark split from a tree yards from the robins. The barrel of the pistol hit Coy on the bridge of his nose. There was a flurry of wings and Coy's vision went dizzy, the birds escaping into the forest. The gun's echo left and everything fell silent. Neither of the sheriffs had moved.

'Did I hit it?' Coy asked.

'Not quite,' said Curtin. 'Why don't you hand me that gun.'

Coy's heart was racing. He held out the gun and dropped it and bent to pick it up.

'I'll get it,' said Curtin.

'Wait,' Coy said. 'Give me one more try at it. Just give me one more shot.'

'It doesn't work that way,' John told Coy.

'That's not fair,' Coy answered.

'It is,' Curtin said, 'and it's not.'

*　　*　　*

In the station house, John asked Coy for Marcy's bond; he was seated again behind the typewriter, at the metal desk next to the window. Night had descended. It was cold in the small room. Coy took his cousin's money out from his jeans pocket, unfolding the creased wad of bills.

'I'm going to handwrite you a receipt for the bail,' John told him. 'You have a month to mail in your payment on the fine. You don't mail it in and you'll have a warrant out on you. Anywhere in Kentucky, they'll haul you in like a fish on a line.'

Curtin had gone down the short hallway and opened the door to Marcy's cell and led her out of it. Coy looked over at her. She wasn't wearing any shoes. Each toenail was painted a different color: bright yellow and lime green, hot pink and dark purple and sky blue. The paint was fading, and had cracked off in patches. Coy thought about Indiana, the long drive, all the towns he'd passed through that he knew nothing of. Once, when Coy was ten, a customer had come to the township's furniture shop with his daughter. The man drove a low black car and his daughter wore a white dress and sunglasses. At first Coy assumed she was blind; a church elder, in his last years, had lost his sight and gone to a doctor and come back with sunglasses and a cane, the second of which he never used, knowing the township well enough to get around without it. He walked slowly but never missed a path's turn or building's threshold, and never once fell.

'Come play with me,' the girl said to Coy, while his father and the other man discussed price.

On the large patch of lawn that separated the shop from the roadside was a see-saw. The girl ran to the raised end of its long plank. She swung the board down and bunched her dress around her, putting one leg on either side of the wood seat. Coy realized she was waiting for him to lift the board level. He walked over to the see-saw's other end.

Together they got the board moving and lifted and dropped, the fulcrum making up for the difference in the weight of their bodies. The sun was behind Coy and he could see his reflection in the lenses of the sunglasses; there were two of him, rising and falling.

'Why do you wear those? Do your eyes hurt?' Coy asked.

'My eyes don't hurt. Movie stars have them,' the girl said.

'What's a movie star?' said Coy.

The girl laughed. 'My dad has three cars but I only like the black one. How many cars does your dad have?'

'We don't have cars,' Coy said, 'we have horse and buggy.'

'I don't like horses,' said the girl, 'I like ponies. Let's play a game. We'll call the game Wishing. Let's wish for all the things that we want but don't have. I'll start. I wish for a pony.'

Coy didn't say anything. He didn't know what to wish for. 'I wish for a see-saw,' he said.

'You have a see-saw.'

'It's not mine, though,' said Coy.

'Whose is it?'

'It's the township's. It's everybody's.'

'No,' said the girl, 'you're not doing this right. Think of something that only you get to have. And you don't have to share it. It's yours, for keeps.'

'Why would I do that?' Coy said.

'Because that's what people do,' said the girl, 'they want things and wish for them and when they get them, they're different.'

'What if they don't get them?' asked Coy. He rose as the girl descended. When she neared the ground she jumped off the see-saw. Coy was dumped to the grass, the wood vibrating beneath him.

'Then they stay the same,' said the girl.

Coy looked at Teshram's money, then at Marcy, then at the sheriffs. 'Keep your receipt and just give me the ticket,' Coy said. 'I'm not paying that bond.'

'That means she stays here,' John told him.

'I known what it means,' Coy said.

Outside, past the station-house door, Coy could still hear Marcy screaming his name. He got in the Torino and took it back out of Loess and drove east, away from Indiana. Ten minutes later, Coy felt for the tinfoil. It was gone from his waistband – he'd lost it. He imagined it sitting in the woods behind the police station or, worse, on the asphalt of the parking lot.

He would have to buy more soon, somehow. He was far

from home, alone on a freeway. He thought of his township's small plots of crops. He thought of the birds flying deeper into the forest. Coy wondered if he'd feel any older by the end of the weekend, when he turned twenty-one. Near stateline the road narrowed and began to descend. Coy crossed into West Virginia, the hills around him turning to mountains.

MICROCLIMATES

The strays will not leave me. I remember them first, now. I remember them before the drive west from Nebraska, the climb in Wyoming, the maddening drop into Salt Lake's odd city and its long lazy flats before reaching Reno, Sacramento and Oakland, and crossing the Bay not the way I had wanted, over the Golden Gate Bridge, but instead by the Bay Bridge, which you deemed pragmatic – *we'll have to save money, I'll have to work hard.*

I was to sit there. It rained forever. It rained more days than it did not. And you chose the Mission because you felt it was needed, that we needed it and that it needed us, that as transplants we had no right to the suburbs – we wanted bombast, the cursing in Spanish, the packed dirty sidewalks, the streets choked with cars. I remember the smell of wet beans in tacquerias. I remember the dive bar just off 15th. I remember your pea coat, your tortoiseshell glasses, your lambswool sweaters, crew-necked and earth-toned. Your chic sneakers of recycled rubber. You wore them down quickly. You were gone nearly always. The back of our building looked out on an alley, a long flight of stairs that led down three stories. We got the good sunlight, of which there was little. We had the top floor.

The first cat was a white cat, white with black patterns, a long pond of black from its shoulders to tail, twin dots of black on both its front paws. He showed up on the back stairs your first week of employment. I never went with you and maybe I should have – taken the CalTrain down to the Valley, you liked the palm trees, *they have lots of palm trees, I thought that they only had palm trees down south.* The stray's eye, its right eye, was covered in pus. I made kissing sounds as I stood in my bathrobe. Three buildings down, a shirtless man watched me. He stood in his window, Korean, mid-forties. When I shifted my leg, the cat turned and ran off.

In Sydney, Nebraska we bought sodas and licorice, and used the black ropes of candy as straws. In Cheyenne, we ate bison burgers. In Elko we fucked in the back of the car. You'd taken your bra off but left on your snap-up. The tiny round buttons were mother-of-pearl, and with my head jammed against the armrest of our butter-colored Volvo I reached up and pinched the snaps on each pocket. *Does that turn you on?* I asked. *We're fucking,* you told me. But I knew it was funny. I pinched and I pinched.

The work that I did – once I had to work, once it was work or go crazy – was drawing these puzzles for games for computers: find all the things in this verdant green jungle or here, in this airplane, or here, in this church. I hid pencils on sink drains, bologna on ceilings, glyphs grapes and slippers on marquees of stores. I'd done the same thing when bored in Art History. Pissarro bored me. Morisot bored me. During Monet and Manet, I didn't show up. In the Mission, I stared out our window for hours, the big streetside window that looked down at the stop for the BART. I'd think about one thing then lose it completely and try to locate it and then find something else. The lights for the traffic wept during rainstorms. The building was old and the wiring faulty; we would lose power for hours upon hours, but by the time you got home it was always back on.

The stray showed up again a week later, while things were still decent, while you and I still went to the shores of beaches, the benches of parks. The new modern-art building was designed to patina, the metal already rusting to green. We took the Volvo over to Oakland and hiked in the hills there, the redwoods prehistoric, our noses turned pink by the sun. The cat sat at the bottom of our long narrow stairwell; it was a kitten and, from what I've learned since then, around ten weeks old. We didn't have kibble or anything like that, didn't even had bread – we always ate out. But we had cereal and milk for our coffee and I dripped the last bits from the slim cardboard carton into a jade-green porcelain bowl. It was six in the morning, a Monday or Tuesday; the Korean man was dancing in the frame of his window, under the bright colored lights of a small disco ball. He saw me and stopped and then kept on dancing. The stray stared at the bowl. I made warm sounds then crouched, the cat turning the front of its body but keeping its head turned toward me, as I edged down and over the lip of the steps. The cat blinked its eyes once – its eyes are emerald – and I set down the bowl and pushed back off the railing and stood on the landing, hope big in my chest.

You worked for a tech firm, the biggest of giants, the word and the thing that made all things happen. I don't know what you did there, after the CalTrain, understood no specifics save for dress code, and when we'd go shopping, an act I found demeaning, you would always make me buy something – some new and striped dress shirt, thin-legged blue jeans, the recycled sneakers just like those you wore. *You have to have something for special occasions,* you'd tell me, *you have to be ready to look more mature.* And we kissed most mornings and fucked on some weekends, but arriving so quickly was roadblock or impasse, our long bouts of silence a string of dark canyons from which we couldn't find our way out. Back home, in Nebraska, your mother was making a quilt. She called us often, asked what we were doing, had we been to North Beach, had we been to that island where they had that jail. She said she'd been reading about microclimates, about how where we lived had pockets and pockets of variant weather, that it could be almost freezing one mile from where it was warm. I talked to her weekly, more often than you did, your purse on your shoulder, your eyes rolling upward, your hand making a mouth. At night, by the TV, your legs tucked up under, your shoes stacked at angles on the worn hardwood floor, I'd dream it was snowing or humid, Nebraska, the green fields of soy plants, the heave of the shocks as the car left the pavement for gravel, for dirt.

The first time that I saw the all-black one was the first weekend that you didn't come home. The back staircase, our staircase, had a fence at its bottom, a gate with a padlock we had no key for. On top was barbed wire. People dealt drugs there, back in that alley, and sometimes were busted, the blue and the red of the lights on our apartment's clean walls. The black one was tiny. One leg had been broken or sprained very badly. You told me overtime, then a convention. The fur on the cat's belly was filthy. The fur, once washed, shone and shone. It stood poised at the bowl, its body stretched out, its eyes looking at me while I stood steps above it. Its brother, the white one, was lapping and lapping. I cooed love words in a tone I didn't know that I owned. The Korean man watched me through his telescope. The device had shown up the previous week. He'd crouch at the lens and then stand up and bend forward, his nose inches from the window. Whenever I waved, he shut the curtains. The all-black stood frozen, its eyes salamander but with more yellow to them, and speckled with brown. Others, before me, had been there and shooed them. I would be different; the cats understood this. The all-black lowered its nose to the bowl.

I hid lamps in car tires, lighters on cupcakes, undersized

zebras on rolled-up newspapers. I was to finish one puzzle a week, but finishing these only took me a morning, and I would go out and wander the streets: up from the Mission and into the Castro and then over to Haight, where I never saw hippies, just lots of stores that sold all the things that hippies made famous: patchouli and patch dresses, incense and bongs. I'd sit in the park on days it wasn't raining, afterward walking west, past Outer Sunset, the row houses painted in bygone pastels. Once at the beach, I would stand at the shoreline. Out on the water were surfers in wetsuits. The waves were too small and the surfers just sat there, bobbing like buoys. I found this disappointing: all these people doing, but doing nothing at all. Some nights I sat on the sand until evening – the walk home in the damp air was over an hour, and there were times you'd arrive back before me, your eyes wide or greedy as I walked in the door, your mind asking questions but your lips unmoving, your cell phone on silent while texts were arriving and I'd walk to our bedroom and hear you click buttons as I shut the door.

There was Oceanfish Dinner, Mixed Grill in Gravy, Chicken and Salmon and Liver and Cheese. There were two preparations, Pâté and Wet Bits. The Pâté was a block and needed dicing. The Wet Bits were shredded and sat in thick gravy. The cats came each morning, on weekends, and nightly. They hung mute on the landing. They knew to be silent. They understood boundary. They waited and waited.

I bought them two blankets that I stacked on each other and set by the porch's back door. A small single window looked out at the staircase, high enough on the wall that you never used it. Nights I couldn't sleep, after I'd set out the blankets, I'd stand on the balls of my feet and peek out it, and the first night I saw them there, sleeping bundled, the white one's paw over the runt's tiny shoulder, my heart weighed nothing at all.

You were promoted. Your workdays got longer. We set the clocks forward. The streets sprang to life. I was at Wal-Greens, buying more cat food. The man from the window, the middle-aged Korean, tapped me on my shoulder, while I was waiting in line. In his red plastic basket were two frozen pizzas. He pointed at them; he didn't speak English. He jerked out two shakes, his chin snapping downward. We walked to his building. The apartment was two rooms with a pullout divider. The disco ball hung from its spot near the ceiling. The shag carpet was thick and maroon and well worn. On his bedside table was a miniature phrase book. He picked this book up and walked into the kitchen, then returned with a pizza, the phrase book still open. He said words aloud in his native language then nodded his head and flipped through the pages. He had on pleated khakis cuffed at their bottom. He had on a white undershirt. His hair was cut short on the sides and in back, but longer on top. I sat down on the carpet, succumbing to the weight of the oddness. Behind me, the telescope's lens pointed skyward.

Oven, he told me. Need Help. Please Cook. The man held out the wrapped pizza to me while I sat there, blinking. Need Help, he told me. You Help. Please Cook.

The dive bar on 15th was called The Nebraska. You and I went there a lot our first summer. The wood floor was covered in sawdust. The stool legs were fashioned to look like cattle prods. There was a brown vinyl booth in one corner; it faced the front door, but sat at an angle where those walking in couldn't see it until they were well into the bar. The game firm I'd worked for had begun downsizing: one more week of projects, then no projects at all. I was sitting at the booth tucked away in the corner when you and the man you'd been seeing came in. He looked to be your age, perhaps a bit older, in his mid-thirties, young but not as young as me. He wore a chic and form-fitting pea coat. He wore on his face a blond, patchy beard, the sort of beard common to white men in the Mission, as though they might hide, underneath it, the amount of their paychecks, the names of their schools. I liked the fact that he didn't seem nervous. I liked the fact that he pulled out your stool.

Our lease was up on the last day of August. The summer was boxes and absence and silence – you'd moved up the hill, into Noe Valley, its sidewalks cleaner, its rent more expensive. All of your neighbors looked just like you. I went up the coast by myself for a weekend, a trip that you knew I was taking, and on my way back came the last text you'd

ever send me: *Stuff's out. Thx for cleaning. Deposit is yours.*
The sofa was gone, the rag rug and the coat rack. In the
bedroom, you'd taken the frame and the box springs and
left our bright mattress there on the floor. The strays loved
the mattress. They set their claws to it. They scratched at
its corners and left their fleas in it. I had bites on my
forehead and bites on my arms. You'd changed your
address but I hadn't changed mine yet, and arriving by
mail in the heat of late summer was your mother's quilt.
I took it out of the box it was shipped in. The background
was mint green and stitched on to this background were
sixteen squares of satin, and stitched on to these squares
were small scraps of fabrics, slivers of cotton in plaid and
in gingham, pink, yellow and blue. Together, these scraps
made a blossom; on each satin background was the head
of a flower in bloom.

There was a night in our only fall there, coming back from
a Thai place just up the hill. You remember this night, yes?
The three men in beanies? How they stopped walking toward
us and paused on the sidewalk? Their black Raiders sweat-
shirts? The tattoos on their hands? I don't know what it was
you thought of in this moment but what came into my mind,
as the thugs looked me over and then spoke in Spanish, and
I in Xicana, and called out as just that, as the first in my
family to be born in this country and now walking hand in
hand with a juera, with a blonde and white girl, was a quote
from Picasso, past seventy years old now: *The value of the*

work resides precisely in what it is not. I talked our way past them, gave you my wallet, turned back around and called them culeros, told you to run. I got home perhaps fifteen minutes later. I had a rib broken, two broken fingers. You put ice in a towel. You asked me why I had to. One of your shoe's heels was missing. You were near tears. Sitting on the table was my brown leather wallet. Curling over its top was part of a pay stub, the final four digits of my SS number. Talk to me, you said. Tell me why this happened. But I sat there and said nothing at all.

It's not that a stray is anything, really, it's that a stray is not something it should be, and for this we mourn.

It was my last week there. You'd taken the Volvo. I'd bought a plane ticket back to Nebraska, to the state that had paid for all of my schooling, had provided the money to sit in a class on Art History, in which I'd met you. A day passed, then two. The strays had gone missing. I'd walk out to the landing and click my tongue for them. I'd bend at my knees, snap a finger and thumb. Night-times I set food out by the blankets, but for three mornings running the food was untouched. I was collecting this food when I saw the sign in the Korean man's window. The man's name is Hyo. The sign said, COME OVER. The apartment's curtains were drawn. Hyo met me downstairs and we walked up three stories, and inside, on the carpet, were the two cats, play-fighting, the all-black so tiny, balanced on his hind legs, pushing a front paw out at the white one. They collapsed together, rolling and hugging. You never knew that they even existed, never once saw their pain and their terror, the joy that they felt from finding salvation. Crying, Hyo said, pointing his finger at me. Happy, I told him, and stared at the cats on the floor.

My dad worked on a soy farm outside of North Platte. My mom worked in a kitchen in town. They are long gone now, back down to the City, always chilangos, both then and still. The woman I married is taller than you are, her skin much fairer, her hair near to crimson. I like how it gets frizzy in the damp air of summers. I like how she never asks about you. We live in Lincoln and have for some years now. Across the top of the mattress, in our spare bedroom, is your mother's quilt.

On the roof of the building that both cats still live in, Hyo has constructed an enormous playground. There are tennis balls, stuffed toys, towers for napping. There are tunnels constructed from discarded duct piping. Hyo rigged chicken wire around the roof's ledges and bolted scratching poles to its flat, tarred ground. When I boarded the plane to fly back to Nebraska, I took a seat by the window, and as we flew east I looked down at the city, hoping, though I knew it was folly, to see the strays playing in the bright and warm sun. Twice a year, Hyo sends me pictures of them in emails. The cats are past five now. The cats have grown up.

EDEN'S

Crumpler had a tire iron and wasn't calming down. The two of us were in the worst part of Fort Worth, searching for a rib place that sold Oxycontin out of its kitchen.

It was midsummer, July, maybe August by then. There'd been no rain all year and now the heat washed over the city each day like floodwaters covering a wide fallow field, muting the streets and making everything shimmer. Crumpler's car had blown a tire on the off-ramp to the freeway. He'd looked in the trunk of his long tan Seville and found the spare flat, taking the iron out of its little cubby.

'Grab the title from out of the glove,' Crumpler had said, and I'd done it. I could feel the piece of paper in my side pocket now, growing damp with my sweat as we struggled down side streets.

'Where do you think we could drink around here?' I asked him. The sidewalks were too narrow to walk side by side, so I trailed behind Crumpler, looking down at his boots. He'd worked at the airport, where I'd been working, too, the both of us heaving other people's baggage onto little conveyors. We'd been pink-slipped the very same day, and since then developed something near to a friendship, the two of us circling the same sets of bars the way that the planes circled the terminal gates, looking for fuel and some brief bit of respite.

'I know when Johnny bonds out, I'll take his spot on the line,' Crumpler told me. He swung the iron into the post of a gate. Grave-looking women in vibrant mumus sat fanning themselves on screened-in porches.

'Okay, but who's Johnny?' I said. I wanted to help.

'Johnny's the future hospital patient who sold me that tire,' Crumpler told me. He stopped and turned around. Sweat flecked his beard's hairs. The skin under his eyes looked rubbed with the same kind of ink that they used to stamp dates into books at the library. 'You don't know Johnny?' Crumpler asked me.

'I don't know anyone,' I said. 'I know you.'

'No, you don't,' Crumpler said, and spun back around and kept walking.

The rib place was called Eden's. We asked and we asked. All of the women shook their heads no and stared at us as we kept walking. Crumpler was coughing like something was stuck way deep down. The neighborhood's stop signs were gone from their poles. Bits of thick glass glittered in the gutters. Not one single car was parked on the street. The blocks were all flat and we could see miles ahead, the road like tarmac under wet, white air that shimmered.

We passed by a brick church gated off at its lawn. Its big

doors were charred and part of the roof had dropped in. Crumpler turned right and I did, too, my cheek meeting his back when he stopped walking. In the building's thrown gloom, in the middle of the street, was a quartet of men standing in front of a cherry-red Nova. Below the car's grille was a pair of women's feet. For a moment I thought that we'd walked onto the set of a movie. A brown paper bag, its sides still sharply creased, lay on the asphalt, a loaf of white bread next to it. One green puckered apple rested against the woman's leg. She had on beige shoes that looked orthopedic.

All four of the men were watching us stare. Crumpler had the sleeves of the airline's work shirt rolled up to his elbows. I watched his forearm's veins bulge under his skin as his hand tightened around the tire iron.

'Whatchu lookin' for?' one of them said. He was shirtless and had a mark on his arm where he'd been branded. Another had on a brimmed hat, its sash the same color as the Nova. The other two wore blue jeans and tank tops and sunglasses.

'Eden's,' Crumpler answered. 'We're looking for Eden's.' On the back of his neck, right over his spine, was a small, round adhesive bandage. Crumpler had worked at the airport for some fifteen years and was older than me by three decades – on the bad side of mid-age, his mistakes more severe, the rest of his life a slow-motion crash landing.

'Eatins?' the man nearest asked. 'You lookin' for food? Walk over here, man. Pick up this apple.'

Crumpler moved his foot slightly over the ground, the sole of his boot scraping some bit of gravel. All four of the men stood up very straight. Part of me was sure that I'd die any second, but most of me believed that I'd never die at all, that when the time came and my number was called, I'd convince whomever was in charge that they'd made a mistake and I could keep on fucking up forever.

'No,' Crumpler said, 'Eden's like the place. Like where one doesn't have to do anything at all and can pretend like nothing ever happened.'

The man in the bright red sash smiled then. 'Okay,' he said. 'I got you. Go back up that street you were on. It's eight or nine blocks and then it's on your left. You'll see a sign sticking out over the street. Say mortuary.'

'Thanks,' Crumpler said, and turned back around, knocking his shoulder into my own while I stood there and stared at the dead woman's feet. The soles of her shoes were little honeycomb shapes. There was a snag in the calf of one of her stockings. The front of the Nova held no damage at all.

'Is this real?' I asked the group of men. 'Are there cameras hidden in the church or something?'

Crumpler had disappeared further down the street. The man in the hat lit a short, thin cigar. 'Come over here,' he told me.

'Why would I do that?' I said.

'To find out if she's real.'

'You mean to find out if she's dead,' I told him.

The man sat down on the hood of the car. He looked at the church, then back at me. 'You can't be real and be dead?' he asked.

'I'm not sure,' I told him.

'Pull her out,' the man said. His smoke hung in the still air like smog.

'Pull her out? From under the car?'

'Yeah,' the man said. 'Pull her out and ask her. Don't you want to know?'

'Not enough to do something about it,' I told him.

Crumpler was a shadow three blocks ahead. The Earth, I was sure, had never been this hot, and would somehow keep getting hotter. Through cracks in the sidewalk weeds grabbed at the air. My little motel room came with a TV, and there'd been a show that I'd watched – *The World Without People*. I couldn't remember how everyone died, but I was overjoyed to see the planet returned to itself, the buildings and asphalt and cars covered with vines and vibrant green grass and bright flowers. It assured all we'd done – the wars and disease, the theft and the lies and the secrets – summed to no more than a thumbprint at the edge of a frame, a clumsy mistake that marred only one shot on a long strip of negatives.

Crumpler waited at a four-way for me to catch up.

'Do the pills that we're getting go well with rum? I want a rum, when all this is over.'

'The pills aren't for you, they're for me,' Crumpler said.

'That seems unfair.'

'Unfair,' Crumpler said. He'd started walking again.

'I came all this way. You can't cut me in?'

'It isn't like that. You've got things wrong.'

'Then you're selling them,' I said. 'It's like a job.'

'Believe me, I need them more than you.'

'So we're *not* going to sell them?' I asked.

'Only if I die,' Crumpler said.

We passed by a house with a porch but no steps. A black bird with a teal sheen to its wings sat shrieking from the ledge of a second-floor window.

'But if you die, how will you sell them?' I said.

'By cutting you in,' Crumpler told me.

At the airport, bags came open sometimes, and seeing their bellies and what they contained was not unlike seeing the insides of a person. Here were the organs of their trip laid bare, shown without context or order – a camera perched on the toe of a shoe, a snow globe, its glass cracked, next to a pair of black leather gloves and a stapler. Looking inside them was like looking into a corpse, each vital thing rendered useless. And above me, near breathless with boredom or dread, in their little round panes, were the passengers. Past the gate, their names called, they sat stiff and mute, thinking ahead to that time when they might walk again, their descent from the heavens finally over.

* * *

The men with the Nova had told us the truth – after blocks of dead trees and wrecked homes and hot street, we saw to our left a thick metal sign that leaned out over the sidewalk. The advertisement was the size of the hood of a truck. Little sockets for bulbs dotted its edges. In precise script of the kind one sees on pharmacy signs was the word we'd been looking for – MORTUARY. Its letters were made out of little glass tubes. Below it were twin windowless doors of blond wood. Crumpler and I walked toward them.

'When we get in there,' he said, 'pretend like you don't even exist.'

'You mean pretend like I'm not alive?'

'That's good,' Crumpler said, looking up at the sign. 'Pretend like you aren't alive.'

'Okay,' I told him.

He pulled the door open and cool air spilled out. A bell tied to the other side's handle banged shrilly. I'd imagined the place made of dark shades and low light, but the inside of Eden's was hospital-bright, with cream-colored tiles and walls painted ivory. The chrome tables were covered in white tablecloths, the chairs' backs in silver-grey vinyl that shimmered. The furniture stood grouped in the middle of the room, as though dozens of people had only just left from a supper. Wadded-up napkins sat on top of sauced plates. A short soda fountain with three silver stools curved out from the wall behind the white hostess station. On the restaurant wall opposite us were two silver doors, a little round window on each of them. A black man with silver hair and white shirt and white pants backed his way through them, spinning around and holding his gloved hands up, his arms for a moment like short, useless wings that sprang from his shoulders.

The man stopped upon seeing us standing there. He looked at Crumpler and then at me and then back at Crumpler, growing his eyes big and walking toward the cluster of tables in the center of the room.

'Eden's is closed,' the man said, making a big pile out of the thin paper plates and walking over to the soda fountain. He leaned over the counter and pulled out a black plastic tub and then walked back to the table, sweeping the plates and the glasses and the forks, knives and spoons into the tub's belly.

'Not for us, though, it isn't,' Crumpler told him.

'You're wrong,' the man said, lifting the tub with both hands. He turned to leave and Crumpler picked up a chair and swung it, the piece of furniture turning in the air before hitting the floor and sliding into the back of the man's ankle. Crumpler was rasping, his breath hissing around in his mouth. Sweat ticked down the back of my neck, past the spot where Crumpler wore his small round bandage. His fingers were still curled around the tire iron's end, and on the back of his hand was a brown-yellow iodine spot.

'Did you just get out of the hospital?' I asked, but Crumpler looked at me in a way where it was like I'd never said it.

The man turned around to face us again, his long arms pulled down by the weight of the tub. He looked upwards, eyes lost to his thoughts, as though he were considering things that he'd put on a list he'd forgotten.

'The guy who makes these decisions, he's gone,' the man said.

'That isn't our fault,' Crumpler said. 'That isn't our problem.'

The man scrunched his face up and bent at the knees. For a moment, I thought he might try to take flight. The glasses from the last patrons' meal made chinking sounds in the tub's plastic belly. 'Please,' the man begged us. 'It's not up to me. I let you back there and things just ain't right. It isn't my job. I just see who's waiting.'

'There must be a way,' I asked, doing this thing with my hand that said, it's okay, the Earth's wrecked, hope's fled, there's just blood.

'There is,' Crumpler said, and then strode at the man with full steps, moving only fast enough to show that he wouldn't stop walking. Crumpler was taller than the busser by six inches or more, so much so that when he swung the tire iron at the man's head it came very close to missing him, and in the second that the long metal rod thudded in, I gurgled, a sound meant to be something more than it was, so puny and worthless in what it offered up it was drowned out completely by the glasses in the black plastic tub breaking as the item fell to the floor, the man following them down in the very next second.

The twin doors at the back of the room slammed into their walls as Crumpler pushed through them. The man's eyes were racing, their lids not quite shut, the pupils pushed up close to his brain so that only two crescents of wet jumpy white looked up at me, and if there are moments where we're compelled to feel, that was when I stepped over the man's half-shaking hand, and walked back toward the kitchen.

I located Crumpler in a closet-sized room, where a time clock hung from a nail on a wall and a short wooden desk took up most of the floor space. Crumpler was crouched down, rifling drawers.

'You're bleeding,' I told him.

'What?' Crumpler said.

'Your Band-Aid,' I said. 'It came off you.'

Crumpler turned his body so he could look up at me, then reached back behind him, smearing the blood from the wound on his neck down close to his collarbone.

'Won't be much more of that soon,' Crumpler said.

'You're getting better,' I said.

'I'm getting over,' Crumpler told me.

I looked out at the kitchen. The chrome stoves were clean. The brown rubber mats on the red tile floor were all spotless. No pots or pans sat unwashed in the sinks.

'What do you mean, getting over?' I asked Crumpler.

'Do you know what your pancreas does? Where it even is?' Crumpler asked me. He pulled a double drawer out of the desk and reached up behind it, grunting as he bent his arm in.

'It's near your stomach,' I said. 'Or your heart. One of the two,' I told Crumpler. 'But I don't have any idea what it does. Do you know?' I said.

'I do,' Crumpler said. He smiled, then slid his hand out of the space where the drawer was. 'It fucks up on you,' Crumpler told me.

Crumpler stood up. He was holding a clear bag full of pills.

'That bag is huge,' I said. 'I could fit that bag over my head,' I told him.

Crumpler grunted again and then walked out of the room, pushing past me and moving over to the long row of stainless-steel tables. He took a single white pill out and crushed it on the clean chrome, damping a finger with his tongue and then touching the digit to the coarse powder. Crumpler tasted the Oxy then zipped the plastic bag up.

'Let's go,' Crumpler said. 'Let's start walking.'

'Wait,' I said. 'So you're dying?' I asked him.

'Man, I am dead,' Crumpler said. 'There's no evac to run. This part's where the black box says the rest. This part's just screaming and fire.'

I stopped walking in front of the silver double doors, and now looked out one of its little round portholes. The man was still there on the floor, a warped ring of dark blood wrapping itself around his head, over the clean white linoleum. His legs bent in a manner like he was trying to dance. There were things missing from me that I knew I should possess, and in that moment I understood that I'd never possess them.

A door with a crash bar was on the far side of the kitchen, and Crumpler pressed it in, turning to shadow. It seemed impossible that there was still sunlight at all. I followed him out into an alley. Crumpler strode toward the street we'd crossed fifteen minutes before just as a pickup, its frame raised a foot, turned in to meet us. The driver's door opened and a thin man jumped down, his cowboy boots brown, white and turquoise. Tucked into his blue jeans was a cream-colored silk shirt, its top button free, the man's brown tie hanging loosely.

'Earl,' the man said, 'what'd you go and do?' Crumpler was still holding the pill bag in the same hand as the tire iron.

'That tire was fucked,' Crumpler said back. 'That whole car's a sham, Johnny.'

'Oh ye of no faith,' Johnny told Crumpler.

I looked at the man for the first time, again, and realized that I had seen him before, on the television. The man standing in front of us was the very same man who owned a lot where they sold all types of vehicles. His commercials came on during *The World Without People*. In them, he wore the same cowboy boots, but he looked smaller now, without his flags and his signs behind him.

The red Nova from before drove past us, out on the street. The man saw us looking and turned his head quickly and then turned it back toward us again.

'This is no place to discuss,' Johnny said.

'Yeah it is,' Crumpler said, dropping the pills on the ground and, for the first time all day, actually running. Johnny took a step backward and caught his boot on the wheel of his truck, turning in mid-step and falling into his door in the moment that Crumpler reached him. There was a small chance the man inside was going to live, but in the salesman Crumpler had found his Great Work, the tire iron coming down as though pulled by some supermagnet. The car title was still in my pants pocket then and I touched at its corner, before running away, wondering when I might be like Crumpler was, too – a loud, sick dog on a long, broken leash, through with commands from its masters.

DOMESTICA

In the photo her back is turned and the light is that late-afternoon light that at least in the photo, and through the white linen curtains, past her, seems self-conscious, shy or otherwise mild, a kind of light that does not want to be there but has accepted itself as having to be there, a sad portion of the capitalized Light, a cast-off bit of light, the aunt without children, the friend who remains unmarried or otherwise without partner, the part of light that enters into any situation awkwardly and wants nothing more than to be gone but cannot be; light that would not be termed bright but has not yet gone gray nor been afforded some bit of color from the impending sunset, flat light, forgotten light, *a dying species of light*, and her back is turned in the photo, and she is standing off-center in the jamb of the doorway to their bedroom, and she has her hands in front of her, near to her chest, in the manner one would when reading a book or saying a prayer or struggling with the clasp on a necklace, some task that requires a bowed head and at least a bit of focus and it is October, in the photo, late afternoon, and they have come upstairs so she can get a sweater, a striped sweater, a horizontally striped gray and orange sweater, a cardigan, the collar of which sits low on her back, pulling down her shirt collar with it and showing fully the pale skin of the nape of her neck, those two inches between the collar and her short blonde hair and because she is wearing the sweater, has it on in the photo and is standing with her back turned to him, she knows that they have lingered longer in the bedroom than the time it would take to just grab the sweater and go, but she has no idea now where they went that day, only that it seemed a necessary thing to get the sweater and put it on before they went, and that in that span of time something else caught her eye or otherwise overrode the idea of leaving, something that involved her hands and a bowed head, but she has no idea now what that thing was.

And the Craftsman two stories with hardwood throughout, Norwegian blond fir he'd imported, sanded onsite by a team of Nez Percé who'd come west from Spokane and before that from Idaho, leapt from the rez and its trenchant malaise, its government food, its gunshots, and she often ate lunch with these men on the porch, brought them sandwiches from the deli of a nearby supermarket as she grew to know and then trust them, and at first they said thank you and nodded their heads and when they trusted her, requests were then added: *I want it on Dutch Crutch, I don't want tomatoes, if we can't have beer I want root beer*, and these men spoke of winter and mothers and death, and one of the men's nephews had killed himself, and had done this by dragging his parents' living-room rug out to State 12 in the middle of night-time, and had lain down on the blacktop and wrapped himself in the rug and had waited there, *rolled up like sushi*, and the other men laughed when the uncle of the dead boy made this analogy, but she didn't laugh and couldn't see how these men might find something like that to be funny, and kept bringing them food but no longer lunched in the shade of the porch, the smell of sawdust hanging about them, and instead took her Volvo to some other place – ran errands or said that she had to; drove east from Ballard up steep narrow streets, past Phinney Ridge into Greenlake, and bought fabric for pillows or some foreign Merlot that she thought would be nice for a Saturday evening, as his work consumed him, and he didn't have time to blindly devote to hand-holding and warm conversation, and one day she came home and the Nez Percé were gone but her thoughts of the boy remained with her, and at bedtime, the lamps off, the room lost to darkness, she pulled the sheets and duvet tight around her, and tried to imagine the night air and hard road and the hum of the truck, getting louder.

And the house is a house that she knew from her youth, had passed by on her long walks to high school, midblock and not special and painted dark blue, the trim somewhere between rust and copper, the brick walk halving the front lawn to twin squares, cordoned off from the sidewalk by waist-high white picket, and here the oak-porch swing, its metal rungs gleaming, and here the braided brass doorknob she polished this morning, and the white-painted door with the circlehead window and vintage brass hinges with figurals of storks etched into their metal, and the side of the hinge that faced out to the street had the stork with its head raised and inside there was the second stork, the stork with its neck curving downward, the stork that did not and would not and would never look toward the staircase that led up to their bedroom and now she must sell it, this house, her address of two years, must sell the stork hinges with the parasol finials, must sell the doorknob and quaint squares of lawn and every other small part of the property: the black latch on the yard gate and fireplace mantel and cast-iron bathtub with wooden block cradle, and the tub was two grand and had shipped from Kentucky and the house held dozens of items like this, things purchased to make their home special, because every square inch was all theirs and should look it, and should not look like it could be anyone else's, and since his work consumed him these choices were hers and she took to these tasks, she enjoyed them, and talked down the tile guy by four hundred dollars and found a chrome-finished range that was perfect, that went with the wall tile and triple bowl sink and flatback toggle-bolted track lighting, and went too with the floor tile and checkered hand towels and near-silent onyx dishwasher, and now these things were things she would not see again, were her things but aren't now, will not be.

*   *   *

And sun in Seattle after so long with none, after three months of rain through the gutters: sun down in Belltown where the white-belted hipsters wore frowns while they ate burritos; sun on the ryegrass at Safeco; sun on the slab docks at Seattle Pier 50, cars queuing for transport in the bellies of ferries, awaiting voyage to Vashon and then Point Defiance; sun on the statue of Lenin in Fremont; sun on the U-Dub Hospital gift shop; sun on the Aurora Expressway – sun in mid-February, miraculous sun, sun so bright it arrives as unwelcomed, and makes too clear each spot on each living-room window, sun that pours in as though it were water, and now she sees patches of dust on the floorboards and where did these come from or how did she miss them as she scrubbed with a toothbrush in each poorly lit corner, as she made her bed then unmade it, tucking the sheets in, the next time much tighter, and cleaned out the self-cleaning oven, and used her compact's mirror to check underneath the interior lip of each toilet, making sure that not one single flake of whatever might have escaped her attention because today they were coming, the buyers, the prospective couples, three couples, each of them interested, and since she's done this herself, without agent or company or help of any kind what-soever, every square inch of the house must be perfect or no one will buy it, no checks will be written, and she'll have to live here through winter and spring and then try again when the days are much longer, when clear skies are constant, and she just can't do that, can't wait in this house for a more proper season, and stare half a year more at the backyard and bookshelves, at the blender and knife blocks and steel empty bowl of the Kitchen Aid mixer, and the curtains she made for the upstairs spare bedroom, their light blue, their sheen, the fabric like silk, so soft that one's hand slipped straight from it.

And in this bedroom's closet a shoebox of photos, flotsam in form of emulsified paper, hundreds of photos and she can't recall placing one of them in the box, ever, nor is she sure where the box might have come from as she owns no shoes by this man, this designer, and the shoebox so full the lid won't close completely, and some of the photos are bound with bright Post-its, and some of the photos are dog-eared, and here is the photo of both of them posed near the door of their favorite diner: pre-brunch, late morning, the last Sunday in April (the date stamped in bright orange in the bottom right corner), and she is two weeks away from a birthday, her third to last before she turns forty, and he has a tie on, and wore a tie always: to brunch and to dinner, to lunch at her parents', to the patch where they picked out their pumpkins, and the ties that he chose were appalling, and the day he found out about her trips to Vashon the tie had been white and green diamonds, and over these diamonds a grid of bright purple, bright purple lines at perpendicular angles and who thought this tasteful *but that's not the aim*, he'd said when she'd asked him about it, when they'd reached a low point and all talk was critique and all moods were some shade of bad mood, *the aim is to stand out and make people remember because once you blend in, you give up, you surrender,* and this had been more than just funny to her – his earnestness was an embarrassment – and in the middle of dinner she'd snorted, had drawn up her napkin to cover her face and issued a chortle into the ivory triple-stitched linen, and across the table, the dining-room table, the cherry wood, walnut-stained, bracket-foot table, part of Broyhill's Louis Phillipe series, he had responded: *I gave you all this and now you are laughing* and she answered *No, we gave us all this,* and *I made these choices, and yes, I am laughing.*

And her friends down in Belltown had all said not this one, and so did her sister and with time her parents, not he of the pockmarks and front-pleated slacks, not he of the Microsoft Business Division, not he who ate meat and commuted to Redmond *by Humvee,* not him, are you serious, but the answer was money, was money and children, and yes he was too thin and some shoes had tassels and there had been talk – he had been truly serious – of a concert on New Year's Eve at Key Arena, a concert by the Quebecoise singer, the hook-nosed chanteuse who defined self-important, and see also: corporate and see also: pathetic, and he, via work, could get third-row tickets, and they would go fast and what did she think and what she thought was this: that's fine, I will go, because we are married and that means being selfless and his tastes will change because we have money and I can take care of keeping things tasteful and we will get older and we will have children, and taste matters less once children arrive and one is caught up in bedtimes and diapers, in play dates and daycare and preschool and grade school, in the unceasing tasks of the parent, and she wrote all her friends off as unrealistic, as they too wanted marriage and babies, and did they all think that the guy they would marry would walk in to the rock club on some Thursday evening and propose between set list and encore, as they just wouldn't – one had to go where these men congregated, and that meant the nice bars more near to downtown, that meant dates to steakhouses, meant giving up one thing to then gain another and now none of these friends had called her in years, had come to the wedding then dropped off the radar, but this wasn't an issue as she had a spouse now, and they had a house, and had money, and once children came the Craftsman as *realm*, a land all their own, the smallest of countries.

The first couple arrives at twelve noon exactly – the bell rings and she is still looking at pictures and the sound of the chime makes her jump and her fingers convulse and she pulls from the shelf the whole shoebox of pictures, and now on the floor, at the closet's threshold, a puddle of image: one half of a photo from a trip to Vancouver covered up by a shot from the deck of a ferry in turn covered up by a shot of her sister, a person that she isn't currently on speaking terms with, and the photo of her with her back turned she takes, tucks into her skirt and with one of her feet sweeps the rest of the puddle back into the closet, and then runs downstairs and opens the door and the couple is smiling and he is enormous, so fat he looks somehow aquatic, and she is tiny; there has to be one full foot of height difference and who were these people and you can't come in here and you will not live in this house of my making, and she needs some air and says let's start outside and walks down the porch stairs and points out the marigolds, did the two of them notice the marigolds, their blossoms of mustard and crimson, and the photo's sharp corner is pricking her thigh, some bit of skin between femur and labia, and the fat man is sweating, and the woman is maybe not even five feet and both of them look like experiments, as though someone had located human spare parts and did what they could with the items provided, and the man's eyes are slats and his nose only nostrils and the woman is waif-like and sallow and pimpled, and she has forgotten to edge the lawn's grass and blades lay limp on the pathway's red brick and she hears herself speaking of vibrancy, that something bright in the garden can counter the winter, can fight off the rainclouds' low ceiling, that marigolds are not only pretty but hearty and the man says we find this all very nice but we aren't big on flowers can we go inside, please.

* * *

Five minutes pass and then ten and fifteen and she grows to feel drugged as their hands move along dirty railings and she listens to the echo of footfalls off ceilings and these sounds, these pedestrian reverberations, make her stomach go queasy, and she moves from her spot by the sink where she's leaning and goes out to the backyard and stands by the apple, the Jonagold that never once fruited, and did not fruit, she found out, because this type of apple relied on a different species to seed it, *it needs some other tree's pollen*, her sister's husband had told her, while they sat in the skybox above the ryegrass at Safeco, watching the Mariners lose to the Yankees, this two summers past, prior to Vashon, prior to waiting in line for the ferry, prior to wrecking two households at once and how did this happen and how did I do that and shame gathers like storm in the sky of her brain, in the deep high blue of her consciousness, and nearby a neighbor has steak barbecuing and she now recalls her first date with her husband, and sitting inside the Metropolitan Grill and her porterhouse being brought to their table, and the steak was almost as big as the plate and she'd laughed and her future husband had shot her a look, a gesture of pure, vitriolic disgust that arrived and was gone in an instant, and she cut at the meat with the wood-handled knife that the waiter had brought her, cut lumps of red flesh and then ate them, and had not eaten steak for perhaps fifteen years and in minutes felt sick but kept eating, kept chewing warm meat while her husband-to-be spoke of Rousseau's Social Contract, that sovereign was false without genuine sanction and union required the quelling of ego and from out of this quelling and union and sanction both parties became indivisible, after which she'd nodded and tried not to throw up as the steak turned to shards in her stomach.

The couple has questions and both come outside and are asking her now about fuses and heating and how loudly the pipes work from behind their walls, *the pipes*, the man says in between rasps, *the pipes*, *are they quiet*, and she says that they aren't, that the pipes are quite loud, that one can hear clearly the rush and the push of the water, and that two fuses have blown since the rains have begun and that once, early on, the basement had flooded, and from somewhere far off comes the bass thrum of thunder and she sees in their faces deflating hope and this makes her happy as she now knows that this couple won't buy and says let's go inside, did you see the couches, and opens the screen door that leads to the kitchen and the three of them walk the floor plan together, traipse the hall of blond fir that runs past the front door and leads into the main room with recessed bay window and here are the sofas of smooth leather, deep brown and uncolored and thereby allowing the leather to breathe better, regardless of climate, and did the two of them notice how well the couches matched with the oversized pink/salmon rug, the hand-knotted Persian, the Lilian rug made by the nomadic Kurdish and did this couple know that these types of rugs were once used as trousseaux, as dowry items, what the wife brought the man to show proof of worth, to signal intent and accept his protection, and that this custom existed since well before Christ, as shown in the code of the king Hammurabi, and the couple are wide-eyed and stare at the floor and the man says they'll call, there are more homes to look at, and she shakes their hands and then shows them the door and with the house empty she draws out the photo of her in the cardigan sweater, and tries to remember what she was holding that day, what sat in her hands, what item.

Because so many items have come through the front door: a brass bed frame, four rugs, eight vases of glass, twin armoires, the nicest of blenders; three tartan blankets of extra-soft wool, platters and teapots and sauce boats and creamers; the digital toaster with extra-lift levers, the wood-framed tile-topped drop-leaf breakfast table; the Eames-era chaise, its curved frame, its six cushions, the upholstered-back armchairs that went with the dining-room table, the pedestal desk in the upstairs spare bedroom, the one they'd replace with a crib, toys and monitor, and what she wants so badly is to become such a thing, to evolve into something inanimate, to sit on a counter or mantel for decades, and gaze mutely at what she's imported, as the plain mirth of life, that dumb joy, that soft warmth, was a concept that always escaped her, and she did not like pets and she did not like laughing and when one was five-ten and when one was size 4, one did not need to be extroverted to garner a surplus of attention – one could be glum and still highly desired, and in college she'd dated professors and doctors, the former encountered through classes at U-Dub and the latter through work at the college's hospital gift shop, and these men had money and many had wives, and bought her boots from Nine West and earrings of diamonds, and took her on trips to Vancouver and Portland, and granted her access to high-end boutiques and taught her techniques of much worth in the bedroom, but once they turned back into boys through the youth she afforded, she promptly dropped them, reminding, each time, of their wives or their titles, should they choose to do something stupid, but none of them did: there were no loud words, no acts one could term as vindictive, and in the long hallways of fourth-floor care wards or brick-walled university buildings, she would pass by them a stranger, all but forgotten.

The next couple is late by an hour then more and she calls the number they gave via email and gets right away the greeting they've left on their messaging system, and here is the man saying the name of the wife and the wife saying the name of her husband, and just as the message is about to wrap up, there comes the jubilant gurgle of a baby, quick happy gibberish, and she calls back eight times in a row just to hear it, the sound of new life, the cadence of promise, joy so pure it defies comprehension, and sits down on the brown and red herringbone ottoman, and hits redial over and over, and stares out the recessed bay window, and how many times has she looked out this window at this span of street, at the trio of elm trees, at the cream-colored Garrison owned by the Burstroms, part of the old Scandinavian guard that family by family was dying, selling their homes for ten times the cost and moving to Flagstaff or North San Diego or Taos or Lake Havasu City, somewhere with dry air and senior communities cordoned off from the rest of society, and her parents, Swedes too, had a timeshare in Tucson, and showing up lately on their breakfast table were high-gloss brochures for accredited living facilities, resort-atmosphere compounds rising out of the mesa with views of not one but two mountain ranges, and these places had bike paths and t'ai chi instructors and ballrooms and Internet lounges, and specialist nurses who dealt with dementia, and counselors that counseled, and showers with railings, as her parents were now nearing eighty years old, and both were still well but no longer drove and no longer went out when the sun was not up and had wondered aloud if the wise thing to do was to pre-empt some minor disaster, and move to a place where care was built in and her answer, each time the topic came up, was you can't move, I need you, and you are my parents.

But her parents were old, and were not getting younger, and needed now to think of themselves first or only, and were not in a place to assist or provide, and were for the first time in her life rather fragile, and because of this did not know the reasons behind both of their daughters divorcing: of her mid-morning trips out to Vashon by ferry, or the subsequent trips to motels in Tacoma, dun ugly lodges within walking distance from the piers and the slips that comprised Point Defiance – of the polyacrylic bedspreads thrown back, of clothes pulled off as though they'd ignited, and her sister's husband was almost six-four, and her sister's husband went rock climbing, and her sister's husband had grown up in Manhattan, and went first to Yale and then Harvard Law and afterward had moved west to protect the environment, gave up his place at the firm in Midtown to stick it to timber and save all the forests, and had done very well and now most of the loggers held jobs at the prisons, the prime moneymaker for so many towns in the tri-state Pacific Coast region, and his house out on Vashon was full self-creation, the floors made of recycled plastics, and lining the roof were blue-black solar cells, and the wood beams near the ceiling were pulled from a fire, and the home's insulation was cotton from blue jeans, and her sister, for work, traveled often, was two years her junior and shorter and wider, more fun but lacking refinement, and this man of New York, this fan of the Yankees, had told her he craved her tact and precision, that women out west were sloppy or lazy, and that she was perfect, and this specific disclosure, told New Year's before last, was something she'd found quite exciting, and now that house on Vashon was gone from existence: the plot sold, the home razed, the driveway jack-hammered, the dirt turning to mud once the weather went rainy.

And now she gets up from her spot on the ottoman and moves down the house's short hallway, and here in the dining room the sheen of the Broyhill, and against the west wall the case for the china – all of it Lenox, the Autumn collection, a gift from his parents, who at one point adored her, slim Californians who lived down in Turlock and made what they could from the raising of almonds, grim sturdy people and he'd been so embarrassed by their ties to the land, by their mother-of-pearl plaid western shirts, by the pace that they spoke, by their pickups and Wranglers, because even with Senate approval of farm bills they would die broke if he didn't make money, and not just enough and not middle tax bracket but the sort of work which afforded him briefcases of money, metal valises with dual-key locks, their insides lined neatly with hundreds, cases that he could attach to his wrist until safely within the high-ceilinged confines of Hummer dealerships and realty offices – a job whose wealth was not quiet – and after their wedding they'd flown to Tahiti, and stayed for ten days in a white-painted villa with white leather couches, and she walked the beaches while he crunched his numbers, as his work consumed him, and while on these beaches she'd pause and gaze out beyond the lagoon to the dark line of coral, and knew sharks swam just past the reef's quick descent, that the water was colder, the light fractured and faded, and after a dinner of swordfish and pilaf they'd gone down to this same stretch of beach and embraced there, hugged as though one of them were going to war and would not be back for a long time, if ever, and the moon on the black of the water was stunning, and he produced from his pocket a 6x9 glossy, and there stood the Craftsman, and not once in her life had she felt so safe, so sure of her place, so calm, so claimed and invited.

And now clouds take the sun and the shadows' sharp lines, and the first specks of mist coat the living-room windows, and what was it she held on that day in the picture and did she still have it and how could it help her, as she wants only to sleep and for things to get better, for someone to come here and repair the damage, but her husband has moved to a condo in Greenlake, and her sister has moved down to Portland, and her sister's husband is back in New York and she knows that her parents will leave for the mesa – that she'll walk once again down dark streets alone and out in the driveway a car's engine turns off and she hears the shutting of vehicle doors and her eyes search the house like the walls were on fire, and here in the hallway the oak antique coat rack, the one that she'd bought at her first estate auction, and next to the coat rack the rosewood wall mirror, and tucked into one of the living room's corners the kerosene lamp from the late 1880s, the egret floor lamp that she fell in love with: its base cold-painted bronze, the bird's body life-size, the metal maintaining patina, the light's globe bright green and adorned with white roses, and perched on each end of the fireplace mantel the twin Sevres vases that she'd bought in Paris, ten inches tall and in rich cobalt blue and mounted on two-inch square-gilded bronze plinths and she'll have to buy boxes and pocked plastic wrapping and stow things securely and hide them away: confine every item to some tiny dungeon, some per-month Elba she'd run like a country while she tried to pretend that she still possessed power, that her items were mighty or would be again, as no land existed without its own customs, without rites that were vogue only inside its own borders, and when one forsook praxis, cast off application, consigned these odd acts to the coffin of theory, one gave up title and castle and kingdom, but she'd allowed long ago for her flags to be lowered, and helped spawn the revolt that had spelled her undoing, and like Huns at the gates the climbing of steps by a duo of beautiful strangers, and now on the porch the day's final appointment, and the chime sounds and she slides off her black leather flats, and then slinks to the door and looks through the peephole, and past the round piece of glass the last wave of marauders: nomadic, exotic, both hopeful and brave (she remembers when she looked just like them), and the chime sounds again and she stands very still and then takes down her skirt and merino-wool tights and draws up her hands to the front of her blouse and undoes, in silence, each button, and then drops the shirt to the blond hardwood floor and what was she holding and how could she find it, and why did the boy take the rug to the highway, and what did he know that she didn't, as the chime rings a third time and her hands go behind her, as she pinches the back nylon straps of her bra and undoes the hook-and-eye closures, and places her hands on her flat perfect stomach, and puts for the last time her eye to the door.

HOW TO STEAL
ELECTRICITY

I'd driven down from Spokane to Gillette, Wyoming because my brother Jed was going to prison, and would be losing his trailer, and wanted me to store a few boxes of his valuables in the basement of the house I owned with my wife. Two months earlier, in March, Jed had beaten a man nearly to death with a pool cue outside a bar-restaurant. When the judge had asked him to comment on his crime, Jed had not – that is, he'd shown no remorse for his actions, and because of this would in a week's time begin serving the full term of a five-year sentence.

The trip had taken half a day. I'd woken up at quarter of six and put the coffee on and taken a shower. When I was dressed and came back out to the kitchen there was pink light pulling itself up the sky in the east, and Janet had toast and scrambled eggs on two plates at the table. Janet and I were going through a rough patch ourselves. Each of us harbored a deficiency. Mine was the fact that my sperm were useless. My wife's was discovering that another man's were not.

Janet sat down at the table in her dull, yellow bathrobe and pulled it tight around her body and cinched the strap around her waist. 'The heat isn't working again,' she said.

'How long have you had it on for?' I said.

'I don't know. Since you got up.'

'Well, it's an older house.'

'It's an old house,' Janet said. She could do this thing with her eyebrows; it made me want to not be there at all. We'd met at a weekend real-estate seminar at the community college three years ago. Janet worked as a receptionist at a law firm, and I did the books for a number of different doctors around Spokane. She was slender and plain-faced, the sort of woman you'd call attractive but not pretty. I was thirty-seven, though, and Janet was twenty-eight. To me, this made her pretty enough.

I looked out the window above the sink. Our home was across the street from a fenced-in park; on weekends, high-schoolers climbed over the fence and took each other's clothes off and left condoms in the grass. Once, a boy had managed to get his pickup inside and crash it into the jungle gym.

'It's an old house,' I repeated. 'Old.' Janet just sat there. She was holding her fork over her eggs the way people at the beach hold a metal detector over the sand.

Ten minutes later, I was in the car. I took our dark blue Ford, a Crown Victoria I didn't trust on long trips, but the minivan still had payments left on it. It was mid-June, and when Jed had called about his sentencing I'd checked in with the different practices to make sure they wouldn't need me for a couple of days, maybe three, though I was hoping it wouldn't take that long. Janet followed me outside.

'I don't want that man's life filling up our basement,' she said. I had the Ford's window down and Janet was leaning inside, palms over the lip of the door. Her bathrobe had opened slightly and I could see the curves of her breasts. They weren't much. I wondered how far I could get the glass back up before she pulled her hands away.

'The basement is much bigger than the car,' I said. Shadows were thinning on the red foothills to the north.

'I'll miss you, too,' Janet replied.

I drove through Coeur D'Alene, Missoula, and Butte, the grasslands giving way to the Bitterroot, then the Rockies. It was a Monday and there were few other cars on the road, and I-90 felt like a thin, black river that had carved its way, eons ago, through the landscape of forest and rock. With its poor banking and swept curves one got a sense that any steering was secondary, that the force and current and gravity of the whole thing was something entered into unexpectedly, and all there was left to do was hold on.

As the highway dipped into a valley near Bozeman, smoke from a controlled burn filled the air and I rolled my window back up. In Billings I stopped for a chicken sandwich from a fast-food restaurant attached to a gas station. I ate in silence at an orange plastic table while children screamed and strips of potato were dropped into oil. When I was finished I wandered the aisles, browsing; from holiday parties at doctors' homes and nights over at Janet's friends' apartments, I'd become conditioned to arrive at anyone's residence with a gift: wine, boxed crackers, an ornament for the tree. The practice is tiresome and obnoxious; I do it every time.

One of the store's aisles was devoted to clothing and memorabilia. There were T-shirts and truckers' caps and belt buckles embossed with the Montana state flag, the Harley-Davidson insignia, pictures of elk or bison or grizzlies. There were bins the size of wastebaskets filled with duck whistles and rabbits' feet, and miniature flashlights one pressed the sides of to make them light up.

At the far end of the aisle, out of sight from the clerk at the register, was a turn rack made of cherry wood. A sign on top of the rack, white with red letters, said: PHANTOM FIREWORKS. Below the sign were packages of firecrackers – Black Cats and Whirlybirds and Spinners that sparked and zipped when you lit them. On the highest row of the rack's prongs were sealed bags of M-80s, each plug of dynamite the size of a D battery. I walked over and put three packages of these in the waist pocket of my blazer, going calmly but quickly to the parking lot, and my car.

I hadn't seen Jed for almost a year, since my wedding. During the reception he'd hot-wired a golf cart and driven it into a water trap and for this Janet would not allow him in our home. We'd postponed our date from January to April because Janet had been in a car accident that had kept her in the hospital overnight with bruised ribs and a broken arm.

The ceremony had been a simple affair at the Justice of the Peace and we were going to have the reception at the park across the street from our house, but the lawyers at the firm where Janet worked had rented for us, instead, the smallest of the banquet rooms at a country club in the rich part of Spokane. They'd included catering, a sound system, a black and white photographer.

I had not been a fan of this idea. In the weeks leading up to the wedding Janet and I had argued, the heaviest of moments occurring over dessert at a Perkins, where I'd swept our plates of Key lime pie and cups of coffee off the table and onto the patterned turquoise carpet below. I am not prone to violence but I am also not prone to charity, and this situation had started something growing inside of me from the moment that I'd heard about it. Janet and I sat across from one another, breathing, while the coffee bled in.

'You need to understand something,' Janet said.

'No, not really, I don't.'

'You will provide me with this opportunity. If you care for me at all.'

'This has nothing to do with providing. This, actually, is the exact opposite of me providing, if you were to lay it down on paper and add it up.'

'Fuck you, Paul, do you know that? Fuck your equations and remainders.'

'I'm still right, though.' The waitress was bent down next us, collecting silverware.

'No, you're not right,' Janet said, lowering her voice.

'How? How can I sit back and accept something like this?'

'Because, Paul, sometimes providing can equal compliance. Sometimes providing means actually doing nothing at all.'

I drove south through Crow land, where the names of towns were just words on maps and nowhere in sight: Garryowen, Lodge Grass, Wyola. I crossed the state line east of the Bighorn National Forest and by the time I reached Gillette it was dusk.

Jed's directions led me through downtown, past lit islands of gas pumps and an all-night grocery and a cluster of hotels, their blacktop lots leading out to the scrub brush and red dirt and just ending. I drove past the Happy Times Bar and Restaurant. Over the door was a neon sign showing a man with a lasso riding a horse. When the sign blinked the horse bucked, its back legs kicking out and up and sending the man forward from the saddle. When I went back to Gillette for Jed's funeral, I remember noticing that the sign was gone.

My brother lived twenty miles outside of town, along an access road that ran parallel with the interstate. His trailer was painted a soft blue that had worn down to a hue close to silver. I pulled the Crown Victoria into the dirt drive, behind Jed's Cadillac, an antique he loved and used infrequently. The Ford's temperature gauge had peeked into the red around Sheridan but the car had been otherwise all right.

All of the lights were on inside the trailer. In place of curtains, flags from the countries Jed had traveled to hung over the short wide windows. Since the Army Jed had made his money playing poker professionally and semi-professionally, meaning illegally. In the mid-nineties he'd placed fourth in the World Championship at the Horseshoe in Las Vegas, but he lost more often than he won and this occasionally left him without any income whatsoever. A recent dry spell had forced Jed to take work at a cattle plant, sorting the usable parts out from those that could not be sold.

I watched my brother's silhouette walk past Australia, Iceland, Japan. Jed was four years older than me; he would turn forty during his first month of incarceration. I had one foot on the trailer's plank steps when he opened the door, grinning. He was wearing denim cut-off shorts, a pair of white flip-flops and a camel-colored chamois shirt, sleeves rolled up past the elbows. His brown beard was fuller than I remembered it, and there was tape covering the left temple of the thick black frames of his glasses.

'You came just in time,' Jed told me. 'They moved my date up; I go in day after tomorrow.'

'How'd that happen?'

'I called down to the judge and said "Move my date up", and he did it.'

'I would have come sooner if you'd told me.'

'I know.'

'Janet said to say hi.'

'No, she didn't.'

I took a second step up the stairs and a sensor light went on, and as my brother bent down to hug me everything went momentarily white.

The door of Jed's trailer led into the kitchen, which was small and immaculate. My brother had learned neatness while enlisted and it had never left him. He'd fast-tracked from PFC to Specialist in eighteen months but this was 1982, and though he'd scored hawkeyes, forty of forty, on nearly every one of his marksmanship tests, he'd seen no live action; it was the Cold War, and there was nothing to shoot at, and instead of a sniper Jed served his country as an electrician. Over the course of his tour he'd been stationed in Melbourne, Reykjavik, and Tokyo. At the last of these bases he'd been flagged for an incident in a mess hall, where he'd put a fork into an officer's leg. Jed had been brought before his sergeant major and first sergeant but he'd received no jail time and just been let go, dishonorably discharged.

The kitchen's floor was polished linoleum, black and white checkerboard with squares large enough to fit both feet on. From an open cupboard above the sink Jed brought down two glasses and a bottle of Old Crow. Next to the sink was a full-size refrigerator, then a small oven. Three identical hand towels, the same red as the chairs, hung squarely over the oven's handle. To my left was Jed's wood-paneled living room. The carpet was a pea-green shag, and in one corner a small television sat on top of a gray metal file cabinet. Old issues of *Life* were stacked neatly on the arm of a black and tan plaid couch, next to a book entitled *Antiballistic Nuclear Missiles*. In front of me, on the table, was an envelope. Drawn next to the laminate window was a picture of a mushroom cloud. The return address belonged to the Department of Defense.

'What's this?' I asked, holding the envelope up.

Jed put the whiskey down on the table. He was grinning. 'You won't believe,' my brother told me, 'what I've got out back.'

When Jed and I were young we used to steal things, petty items that we consumed or quickly lost interest in: dime-store candy, a single glass bottle of Coke, a pair of work gloves left on someone's front lawn. We were never caught, never even came close, and if we were stealing from a store we always bought something along with what we took, both to cover our tracks and make up for our wrongs.

In high school Jed started stealing electricity. This act had arisen from need; our mother had run off to Colorado with a man who bought bankrupt farms and our father was a drunk, someone who spent what free time he could in places where good lighting was not desired. Paying the gas bill was low on his list of priorities. My freshman year of high school – Jed's junior year – our house's power was shut off. This was the same time, also, that the FDA discovered a steroid being giving to cows, to increase the yield of their milk, was causing rats in university laboratories to grow blind or get cancer or, in some cases, render them sterile. Once, I showed this study to Janet. She'd read the whole thing and then thrown it in the trash can, with no words at all.

Jed had a part-time job bagging at a grocery, but my father owed hundreds of dollars, perhaps a half-year of bills, and when he came home after nine hours at the Boeing plant and another five at the bar to find the light switches strictly ornamental, he'd gone to sleep on the couch without a word about it. After a week of no change, Jed solved the problem himself. He learned what he needed to from our Shop teacher, a retired engineer named Mr Spitz, a nice man who was eager to answer questions without thinking about what his students might do with the knowledge gained. During class one morning my brother had raised his hand and asked, simply, how the meter man rigged up power to a house, and how he checked how much energy that house had used. And in layman's terms – expert but easy to follow – Mr Spitz explained to my brother diodes and amperes, anodes and siemens, impedance, reactance and superconductivity for the four hours after school had let out for the day. Jed came home past sunset (it was mid-October, and getting cold) with a bag from the hardware store and told me to turn all the switches on inside the house, then get a flashlight and come around to the back.

Following my brother's instructions, I spotlighted the lock on the meter's box and my brother jimmied it with a screwdriver until it broke open. He swung the gray door back and went to work. On the ground next to him were the contents of the hardware-store bag: needle-nosed pliers, two coils of electrical wire, and a thick roll of duct tape. It was before nine and too early for our father to return and surprise us. Our home was on the outskirts of Spokane, its backyard looking north toward Buckeye and Deer Park and the Kaniksu National Forest. Since my childhood new development has filled that expanse of land but the house is still there, re-shingled and freshly painted, and some Sundays, when I go for drives, I pass by it.

I moved around and stood behind my brother, in order to better light his work. In two minutes he'd taken the meter's face off, exposing a brain of wires and circuits. With the pliers Jed stripped two of the wires' rubber casings, then pulled them away from the rest. Stars glowed in the clear sky. Our breath shone in the cold. Jed made a sort of bridge between the old wires and the lengths that he'd bought, taking a step back before completing the patching. There was a pop, then a spark, and then all the lights in every room of our house came back on at once.

Behind the trailer was sagebrush and rock and Wyoming blackness, a sort of dark that made me feel obsolete, not a part of anything. Jed was bent down, hand-cranking a generator. He'd brought out two flashlights, both with compasses built into their bottom ends. After some moments my brother flipped the generator's switch and a floodlight illuminated the night.

'Something to guide us back,' my brother said, checking and rechecking his flashlight, and handing the second one over to me. 'Don't turn it on yet, if you don't mind, Paul. Wait till we get farther back from the road.'

'Where is it we're going?' I asked.

'Out there,' said Jed, pointing to the empty space ahead of us.

'Why?'

'Because this is the last chance I have to show you something, before it's not there anymore.'

My brother started walking out into the night. I followed him. In the sky was a true blanket of stars, unaffected by the glow of cities, a wash of celestial brightness that turned the black space around them to blue. I'd left my jacket in the car and now wished that I had it; while the spring days were warming, the nights were still cold. After a half-hour of following the sound of my brother's flip-flops over the rocks and dirt, Jed stopped and flipped on his flashlight.

'Check your compass,' my brother told me, turning the light on my hands. I did what he said.

'Perfect north?'

'Perfect north,' I said. Jed shut his flashlight back off. We kept going.

Forty minutes later I noticed, for the first time, a row of orange dots in the distance. I knew this would be our destination, though I had no idea what it could be. The floodlight Jed had left on had shrunk considerably now, a small bright thing behind us.

'Do you see it yet?' my brother asked, not stopping walking.

'I see something up there, ahead.'

'What do you think it is?'

'A filling station for mining trucks. An illegal casino.'

'Wrong on both. A casino would be great, though. I'd walk this stretch every night.'

After perhaps a mile more we reached a chain-link fence, a vertical barrier in the middle of nowhere. Around the top of the fence were looped rings of cyclone wire. Signs, at regular intervals, were bolted to the chain links. They read: UNITED STATES AIR FORCE PERSONNEL ONLY. DANGER. PELIGRO. KEEP OUT. There were no people or vehicles anywhere in sight. Jed switched his flashlight on; in the beam of light his breath looked like smoke.

'What is this place?' I asked my brother.

'It's a missile base. Next week they're blowing it up.'

I looked back inside the complex. Six low buildings with sloped, aluminum roofs stood near the other side of the fence, wide and silent and white. A cement road led into the base on the fence's far side, circling the perimeter. In the center was a square of trimmed green grass, the size of the park across the street from my home in Spokane.

A small slab of asphalt, like a miniature runway, connected the road to the lawn's center, stopping at a steel door built into the ground.

'They're going to blow the missiles up?' I said. 'Right there?'

'The missiles never get blown up,' Jed told me. 'The Air Force just decommissions them and takes them somewhere else. The bases, though, they do.'

'Where do they take the missiles to?'

'Montana, usually. Or North Dakota. They have fields devoted to this, acres of land. They were going to start another one in Nevada, but they decided that was too close to the coast.'

In the plains' stillness I could hear the hum of the base's lights, the filaments buzzing in their heavy-duty bulbs.

'How did you know this was going to happen?' I asked. My brother had his hands hooked through the fence now, fingers curled around the links. I imagined him standing like this in prison, face close to the bars of his cell, only the smallest parts of him able to break their plane.

'The government had to send a letter out to residents,' Jed told me. 'So no one would think it was the real thing. They're detonating next month; you should come down and watch it. They contract out a demo team; it's gonna be the first and the last time this place sees any action.'

'I don't think I can make it down again in a month, Jed.'

'I know,' said my brother, 'that's why I brought you out

here now. What you see before you,' my brother now told me, sweeping his arm around, 'is dying proof of a lack of nuclear war.'

After her traffic accident, while she was still in the hospital, Janet had had a miscarriage. Her doctor was a young East Indian named Rupert who spoke with a British accent. He was taller than me, with long hair that he wore in a casual manner. Under his white lab coat, he had on a collared denim shirt and khakis. While he spoke to me he kept his gaze on the ground, as though he were reading from a script that had been left there.

Janet had rear-ended another car at a moderate rate of speed, this man explained, and the collision had been forceful enough to throw her body into the steering wheel, breaking her humerus and causing spontaneous abortion to occur in the womb.

'Did you know that you were pregnant?' the doctor asked me.

'No,' I said. 'I did not know that we were.'

The two of us were standing in a long white hallway outside Janet's room. It was just after New Year's and Spokane was under a foot of snow. Janet and I had bought the house across from the park the summer before and I was at home, working, when the police had called to tell me where the paramedics were taking my wife.

'Will she have problems having babies later?' I asked. The

doctor said she should not. He asked me about Janet's family history. I told him both of her parents were deceased, that they'd lived in Moses Lake, to the west, their whole lives. He made a note of this on the piece of paper on the plastic clipboard he was holding.

'How long?' I asked.

'Pardon me?' the doctor said.

'How long was the baby inside her for?'

'At most eight weeks. Not past the first trimester, certainly.'

I looked through the small reinforced window in the door of the room where they were keeping Janet. She was on her back, sleeping. She didn't have any tubes in her, but there were two round Band-Aids over the inside of her forearm, and I could see a cut just above her jaw.

'If it's something you're concerned about we could schedule a fertility test, to make sure everything's functioning normally.'

'I'd appreciate that,' I said, still staring at my wife.

'When would you want to make an appointment for?'

'Is it possible to do it tonight? Right now?'

'I'm afraid it's too soon after the accident to perform anything like that.'

'No, not on my wife,' I told Rupert. 'I'm asking can I take one myself.'

At home, on occasion, when I'm taking a break from doing other people's taxes, from adding everything up, keeping everything accountable, I look out the window above the sink and think how badly, for a short while, the boys in the park would want my condition, would pay good money to guarantee that no offspring would come from their drunken night-time fucking, condoms like bullet casings lying in the grass.

I am not a happy person; I know this about myself and I accept it, having conceded that there is, most likely, something chemically wrong with the part of my brain that determines and regulates joy. I wonder, sometimes, how much of people's lives are governed by this single thing, joy, and the weighing of their own against another's.

And I wonder sometimes, too, about what the man Janet slept with might have looked like. I cycle through the same set of faces: the lawyers at the firm; the doctors for whom I work; male friends that we both have in common. It's true that there could have been more than one person, could have happened more than once, but I don't believe this to be the case because on some level I like to think that I know my wife. Either way, and whatever their numbers, over the years I've assigned him or them a single body, absent of detail, or, rather, with mutable details. I will be standing in line at the grocery or dropping off forms to a desk nurse in a hospital lobby and there will be a man in line in front of me, or sitting in a chair, reading a magazine, and I will think: you are the man who slept with my wife and impregnated her.

For her birthday, the year that I drove to Wyoming twice, once to see my brother alive and a second to see him dead, I taped a Xeroxed copy of the results of my fertility test to the inside of a Hallmark card and had a courier deliver it to Janet at her work. On the inside of the card I wrote a short note: WHAT HURTS ME MOST IS HAVING TO REMIND YOU OF SOMETHING YOU'VE ALREADY DONE.

I slept dreamless sleep on the plaid couch in Jed's living room after we got back from the missile base, and woke at dawn to the sound of the trailer's screen door slapping shut. I got out of the sleeping bag I'd brought with me and walked into the kitchen. Last night's whiskey glasses had been cleaned and put in the drainer next to the sink. In their place were two empty mugs and a pack of blue Aviator cards, the seal unbroken. On the counter next to the stove, coffee had started to drip into the maker's glass pot.

I could hear my brother singing from behind the trailer. I went over to the window and drew back the Union Jack, the orange morning light coming over the checkerboard linoleum. Jed was wearing the same clothes as the night before and looking through a pair of binoculars in the direction of the silo. The song he was singing was from an Army marching drill, one I recognized but didn't know the name of.

The trailer's bathroom was off Jed's bedroom, which had

the same pea-green shag over its floor. The only furniture, aside from my brother's single bed and an emptied bookcase, was a small oak desk. Jed's Remington, a 16-gauge Wingmaster, leaned against it, the stock broken and the barrels empty of shot.

Along the ledge of the window were small bottles of shampoo and still-wrapped hand soaps Jed had taken from the casino-hotels he'd stayed in over the years: the Ray in Helsinki, the Grosvenor in Nottingham, the Spielbank Bad Kissingen on the fringes of Germany's Black Forest. Caesar's Tahoe, the Borgata, the Bellagio. The Aviation Club De France. Next to the bed were three cardboard boxes, duct-taped shut. On the side of each, written in black marker, was the word SPOKANE.

After two months with free power my brother and I got caught. A policeman showed up at our door the week of Christmas, late in the afternoon. My brother and I had the television on. The dishwasher was running and the radio was playing upstairs. Holiday bulbs, green and yellow and red, were wrapped around the arm of the banister, blinking; our father had forgotten about a tree.

Jed was the one that answered the officer's questions, which were not, initially, in regard to our tampering with the meter box, but rather about an Olympia beer sign we'd taken the previous day, a cumbersome thing we'd found in an alley on our walk home from school. When you plugged the sign in, the word OLYMPIA lit up in gold neon, and a waterfall, painted onto the sign's face, glowed from the underside in such a way as to make the water look like it was moving, cascading down from where the river ended above.

The sign, it turned out, was not discarded but a newly purchased item, dropped off at a back entrance of a bar. It had been my idea to take it. My brother didn't mention this as he talked things out with the cop.

'We can get it for you right now,' Jed had said. 'We didn't know anybody needed it.'

'If you do that we can forget about this whole thing, but with your permission I'd like to look around upstairs and behind the house, to make sure that's all you've taken.'

'We're telling the truth,' my brother assured him.

'Then there's nothing to hide,' the officer said back, leaning in over the threshold. From our bedroom, Bing Crosby was singing about mistletoe.

'Well, if I show you another thing will you promise to listen to the whole story, all of it?'

I was sitting in front of the television, not watching it, trying to come up with something to say. I can't imagine how different things would be now if I'd just found the nerve to speak up.

'That depends on what you have to show me,' the officer answered. From the corner of my eye I saw his hand move to the handle of his baton.

Half an hour later, this same man put Jed in handcuffs and three months after that, instead of going to jail when he turned eighteen, Jed was sent to Basic Training at Fort Bragg, in North Carolina. His statement to the police mentioned me only once, to say I was at a friend's house when Jed broke open the meter box and sent thousands of watts hurtling through the copper veins of our home.

We took my Ford to Happy Times for Sunday brunch. The restaurant was next to a Best Western, which was next to a Day's Inn. There were more hotels beyond that, too, a stretch of them along the same four-lane road that bisected the interstate, hundreds of rooms that people would stay in one night or two, or until their credit was tapped and their worth ran out altogether.

After a bad loss in Helena, Jed had worked as a maid at one of these hotels, though he'd never said which. For three months he made beds and cleaned toilets until quitting mid-shift and driving to Denver and winning fifteen thousand in a tournament. Afterward my brother phoned to tell me the details of his winnings, but I could think only of what he had lost.

The restaurant's lot was almost full, and we'd had to search before finding a spot. Inside Jed and I were seated at a booth near the window. Families in church clothes and groups of Crow men and long-haul truckers filled the tables and stools at the counter, talking and eating. As I was looking at the menu a sound filled the room, and I didn't realize until I looked up that the din was applause for my brother; people at some of the tables – a lot of them, actually, twenty, at least – had coffee cups or glasses of juice or soda or water held in the air, and they were hitting them with their forks and knives and spoons. A cook came out of the kitchen and banged the heads of two metal spatulas together. The clientele, in its entirety, was staring at us. I looked down at my place mat. In bright yellow letters with brown outlines, the piece of paper read: GILLETTE: BIGGEST TOWN IN NORTHEASTERN WYOMING.

'You've got a fan club,' I said.

'Last supper,' Jed answered, hitting his own fork against his empty mug and adding to the noise.

My brother had beaten the man he did, a traveling salesman from North Platte named Timothy Richards, because Richards had cheated at a hand of seven-card stud. The game had taken place in the bar portion of Happy Times on a Wednesday night, with Richards, at the end of the hand in question, standing up from his chair in his black pinstriped suit and white shirt and tie and showing a flush, five diamonds, on my brother's three nines. Jed and the salesman were in a group game with two waitresses, a volunteer fireman, and a state trooper, all of whom had three or four beer bottles apiece standing next to their stacks of chips. Everyone was down except for Richards, who was making out big.

'Something's going on here,' Jed had said, staring at the man's diamonds. 'Something's a little off, I think.'

'Could be,' said the state trooper, fingering his beer bottle.

'That's lies and you know it,' said Richards. 'My luck's running high and you're giving me shit on account I'm not local.'

'That could be, too,' said my brother, 'but didn't your hand kind of swing to the side a bit that last deal? Hey, Stu,' my brother said to the fireman, 'did you notice this man's index finger slide over to the side of the deck when those last cards were coming out?'

'I think I did, yeah,' answered the fireman, 'I think I saw his index finger slide over some.'

'The Electrician's Grip,' my brother said.

'The Electrician's Grip; yeah, I think I saw him do that.'

I hadn't needed to stop Jed at this part of the story, as he related its details to me. From our previous conversations I knew all methods of cheating at cards. Janet knew them, too; my brother had explained them to her for an hour at our reception, before getting drunk and bored and finding a golf cart behind a maintenance shed next to the sixteenth green.

'This is bullshit,' Richards had said, more loudly, 'and I'm close to the Lord's name in vain.' He looked around the table for support to his claim and, finding none, turned his stare back to my brother. 'I don't know what kind of sorry life you people have had but there's no need to take it out on me. You're in this together, all of you; you're just trying to steal my juice.' Richards put his hand over the money and started pulling it toward him.

'That's not true,' my brother replied. 'I'm only trying to keep what's rightfully mine. And I'm pretty sure that money doesn't belong to you. I'm pretty sure that you're not goddamned getting out of here with that.'

'I'm into Grand Junction by sunset tomorrow,' Richards answered. 'I'll tell you what.'

'Let's calm it down now,' said the trooper.

'We're leaving,' said both the waitresses.

'I'm leaving too,' said Richards, grabbing most of the cash from the table and putting it in one of the pockets of his suit. My brother waited for the salesman to exit Happy Times before walking past the bar's only pool table and taking one of the warped, scarred cues down from the wall.

'I'm radioing this in,' the state trooper told my brother. 'Stop it, Jed, right now.'

Jed had offered no response whatsoever; he'd simply opened the door to the parking lot and went outside.

It was the fireman, Stu, who saved Richards's life, tackling my brother after he'd beaten Richards unconscious. Jed sat cross-legged on one of the parking lot's cement blocks, his fingers interlocked on his head. He hadn't taken the money from the salesman's pocket – that was not the point, he told me – and the witnesses explained things in such a way as to keep the graver charge of attempted murder out of the picture.

Richards himself, perhaps out of fear of retribution, or because he had been cheating and knew he was in the wrong, refused to say that the incident was anything more than an argument over a game of eight-ball. They'd taken his statement in the ICU of Gillette Memorial after he'd regained consciousness, and he'd been allowed to testify via closed-circuit television from a courthouse in Nebraska, one state away.

'The waiting there,' my brother told me as we finished our breakfasts, 'that was the hardest part. Knowing what had happened, and waiting to see what was going to happen next. That being stuck in between.' Jed unscrewed the cap on the glass jar of syrup and poured the rest of it onto his plate, using his final pancake to mop it up.

We spent the rest of the day in Happy Times, moving back to the bar after we were finished eating, and drinking bourbons with Blue Ribbons until the sun went down. At one point, a woman named Kelly, who worked dispatch for a concrete company and had been sitting with us and drinking on our tab, offered to let me follow her into the bathroom. She'd proposed this plainly and evenly and at a normal volume, had stated simply that I could join her while she went to freshen up.

I'd almost accepted, too, and would be lying if I said there weren't moments since that I wish I'd stood from my seat and gone with her. What stopped me was wondering if Janet's affair had been like this, had occurred or at least begun at some random establishment on an average Tuesday evening, her faculties impaired, a warm body offering itself up.

I didn't follow Kelly to the bathroom because I knew that if I did I would one day tell my wife about it, and that we would share the same horrible privilege of knowing that the person we'd married had, for a short time, forgotten what that was supposed to mean. Debt lives most fully in the burden of memory, rather than the minutes or hours in which it is incurred.

'It's your loss,' Kelly said when she returned to our table.

'Yes,' I said, 'it is.'

The sheriff came the next afternoon, followed by a deputy in a second cruiser. We waited for them on the trailer's plank steps, my brother and I drinking glasses of pink lemonade.

'Did you know those golf traps are made of cement?' my brother asked. 'The ones at the country club?'

'No, you never mentioned that.'

'They were covered in algae, too. Took me a half-hour to get out.'

'That must have been tough.'

'It wasn't so bad. It was the only time I've been in water at night. And there were so many glow bugs. You remember the glow bugs? It was like swimming under lights.'

'What's going to happen to your Cadillac?'

'Ernie's coming to get it; he's going to hold on to it for me. The gun and the furniture, too.'

'But he couldn't have kept the boxes?'

'He could have.'

'Then why did you need me here at all?'

'I didn't. I just wanted to see you. And to have you see the silo, before they blew it up.'

The day was warm and I could feel summer in it, the sagebrush wanting to bloom.

'Your car's a piece of shit,' my brother told me.

'It's old. It's a '90.'

'You should buy a new one.'

'We did. We bought a minivan.'

'You should have brought that. Would have gotten better mileage. Could have saved yourself money on gas.'

'I can't risk it,' I told my brother. 'It still has payments left on it.'

'But the old guy,' Jed answered, 'the old guy's expendable.'

'I'm sorry that I haven't come down here more often, Jed.'

'It doesn't matter.'

'It should, though.'

'It should, maybe, yeah.'

And then I remembered. 'I brought fireworks,' I said. 'I stole them from a gas station. M-80s.'

'Quick,' Jed answered. He was smiling. 'Get them quick. Right now.'

For the next forty minutes, with the silo's buildings in the distance, my brother and I took turns lighting firecrackers behind his trailer, waiting for the hiss of the fuse to begin before flinging them upward as hard as we could. We laughed out loud with each new explosion, my brother's cackle a lost boyhood remnant returned. Jed gave me the last one but I gave it back to him. He held the salute over the flame of his Zippo, grinning at me as the wick started to sizzle. Jed heaved the shell toward the Wyoming heavens. One second later, it burst into nothing. Puffs of black smoke hung in the sky then were gone.

Both the sheriff and his deputy wore hats with bolos around their brims and reflective sunglasses, their lenses mirrors in which I watched my brother and I grow bigger the closer the two men came. For the second time in my life I saw my brother get arrested, the officers dressing him in handcuffs and leg shackles before leading him down the steps. There was only a short length of chain between the iron over Jed's ankles, and this gave him a constrained way of stepping. It made my brother walk like he was hurt. As they guided Jed into the back seat, he held up his cuffed hands and gave the only smile he could muster, a weak thing far short of a grin.

I can't remember the cruiser pulling away, but I have a singular dream on occasion of Jed trying to climb out of the water trap at the golf course and saying, over and over, *Ernie's coming to get it; he's going to hold on to it for me.* The dream disturbed me at first but with time I've grown used to it, as I have with a great number of things.

My brother died two weeks after starting his sentence; he bumped into someone he shouldn't have in the recreation yard, and for this two men carved the ends of wooden rulers to points and stabbed Jed in the face and the throat and the stomach. They did this in the middle of the cafeteria, while lunch was being served, and having kept to himself in prison, as he had done for most of his life, my brother bled out on the linoleum floor, with no one around who would help him.

Janet and I still live in Spokane, in the house across the street from the park. We will never have kids, are too old to have kids now, and times she's at work or out running errands, I consider how our lives might have been different were the rooms of our home to have filled with the marvelous salvos of children, their volleys of laughter like bright detonations. Instead, I exist as the last of my bloodline, a glass bulb blacking from tungsten, a switch waiting to be forever turned off.

NATIONAL
TREASURES

In which the Seller commodifies his dissent, listing for the first time this previously uncollected compendium of National Treasures, the delimited choices most chiefly informed by the Seller's belief that each person is a country unto themselves, and possesses a record of conflict and treaty, has customs and boundaries and scandals and ways – that every small piece of the self is worth something, and too that the Seller is broke, and can no longer afford the small storage unit off the Queens Midtown Expressway, Exit 15, and for nearly two months has been receiving, by voicemail, threats from said storage unit's owner, a Sikh, one Mr S. Bedi who has promised to heave all of the Seller's belongings out into the street, and so then this cyberboutique *sui generis*, its governing tenets lying ultimately between Organic Nationalism and Dynastic Hegemony, between amour de soi and amour propre, an emporium that's sought to accommodate too much, and whose ruler now seeks to sell off part and parcel. These items are priced to move.

Lot of Children's Winter Clothes: Two Parkas, Eight Ski Hats, Four Pair Mittens, Two Pair Sorrel Boots, Child Sizes Ten and Six, Respectively.

Born in Buffalo to middle-class parents, September 1975, my younger brother followed me from my mother's womb some twenty-seven months later. We lived mid-block, between a divorced beat cop and a semi-professional painter named Janine Bench, who was in her fourth decade while I lingered in pre-pubescence. Winters were maelstroms of snow; there were consistent stints of no electricity, and people began buying firewood before Labor Day. I can recall watching Miss Bench painting by candlelight; the bedroom that I shared with my brother, Chase, had a window that looked out at her studio. My neighbor was a gaunt dishwater blonde with mild features, save for a rather pronounced chin, which made her profile unintentionally comic. She was naturally attractive but put little stock in her physical appearance, spending most of her time around the house in the same cocoa and pink velour robe, a neck-to-feet item that she rubber-banded the left sleeve of when applying paint to canvas. I imagined her rich, even though she lived right next to us and we were most certainly not, my mother working clerical at a Federal Building downtown and my father teaching math at Grover Cleveland, the public high school I would later attend. Miss Bench worked days at Oliver's, one of Buffalo's standout restaurants. I realize now that the reason I thought her wealthy was that her lifestyle was different from most people's, that she was most generally 'other', an idea I was fascinated by: that there was always the anti-, the un-, lurking nearby, stockpiling. I spied on her whenever I could.

Nearly all these people have passed from this world: the beat cop got shot, Miss Bench had a stroke, my brother jumped off the roof of a building five blocks from Manhattan's Port Authority Bus Terminal. My mother, too, is gone; she bought Kents by the carton, vowing always to quit. During one no-power stint in deep winter, I was sent down the block to procure more of these, the corner store, thanks to a generator, open through the worst. Miss Bench was at work and did not lock her door and I had failed to keep my curiosity (innate) quelled sufficiently. That is, I turned the handle and went inside. Miss Bench's front room held no furniture; she utilized the space as an ersatz gallery – paintings hung everywhere, large canvases in grays and browns and blues. Later I would realize these as poor imitations of the 'Ab-Ex' tradition: destitute imitations of the work of Rothko and Kline, lots of lines and boxes, the hues chosen most certainly influenced by the torpor of Buffalo winters. I took nothing and left, not realizing that my boots (the larger-sized Sorrels listed above) had tracked in snow from Miss Bench's front steps, thereby indicating that a stranger had entered her house. Through high school she offered me only terse waves and sideways glances, acts that left me feeling wholly guilty, despite the fact that I had done nothing, really, wrong.

Starting Bid: $9.99

VHS Recording of Rogers and Hammerstein's *Oklahoma!*, as Performed by the 1987 Sixth Grade Class of Phelan Academy. 72 Minutes. Shot with a Panasonic Dual-Head Hi-Fi Camera.

Being in education and realizing that the extent of Reagan's concern, in regard to public schools, hovered somewhere between 'fuck' and 'you', my father enrolled me at Phelan Academy, a non-sectarian private institution that sat on the east end of Buffalo's west side. I attended Phelan from third through eighth grade. In the fourth grade, a librarian stabbed another teacher upon discovering the tryst between the stabee and the librarian's wife. The following year an ex-Bills linebacker wandered onto campus, high on PCP. (Later, while a sophomore at SUNY-Albany, I would better attempt to understand my brother's own addictions by trying this exact receptor antagonist in a friend's dorm room. The effects upon my person were not dissimilar to swimming in drool).

There was a second performance of this musical that wasn't taped, performed at some other school very deep in the ghetto, a place whose name I cannot remember. I and my classmates, less concerned about performing with any legitamcy sans the attendance of our parents, had located in the men's dressing room a bright orange inflatable ball, which was taken by me or one of my cohorts from said dressing room and released onto the stage during a meager rendition of 'The Surrey with the Fringe on Top'. To say our chaperones – comprised of three teachers, including the drama teacher, an aged hippy with the first name of Splendor – were indignant would not do justice to the rage that they held inside them, and had to keep holding inside them for the full duration of the play, until the production was over, at which point a half-dozen of us were repaired to a vacant classroom and beaten savagely, boxed around the ears and held over knees and spanked, the last of these minor tortures both painful and embarrassing, as we were really too old for this particular mode of punishment. I can only imagine how this meting-out later affected the sex lives of my cohorts, but I now admit fully a predilection for slapping firmly the bare rear of every single partner of intimacy, of raising my hand and then lowering it, and thereby leaving upon a half-dozen individuals misdirected acts of revenge. Opening and closing credits included. Intermission partially edited out, though as the camera comes back on you can see clearly my brother, age nine, stop, just for a moment, in front of the lens. Slight wear marks in this section of the tape due to repeated pausing. Performance Itself is Unflawed.

Starting Bid: $4.99

Lot of 2 (Front and Rear) State of New York License Plates, 1973–1986 Era. Plates are Gold with Blue Letters: 8675-KKY.

Stickerless: Window Validation. Front Plate Creased (See Below).

Unable to afford Phelan for the final stage of compulsory schooling, my parents enrolled me at Grover Cleveland High School, ten blocks from Lake Erie and the Canadian border. Occupying a full city lot, the school, erected in 1913, is in the Colonial Revival Style of the period: symmetrical façade, pediment supported by pilasters, voussoirs, etc. Steel-framed, with a stone, red-brick and terracotta exterior, this cupola-with-spire-topped hellhole was where I would first make the acquaintance of one Frederick Ames Kemper, cast, like myself, in a non-speaking role in the drama that was Grover Cleveland's junior varsity football team. The misery of the bus rides to away games approaches the indescribable: I was lithe and asthmatic, and tormented with a sort of passion I can only term Roman. Everyone smelled like wet, dirty socks. But there also, in that rage-drenched miasma, Frederick: flaxen-haired, halcyon, a toiletries bag filled with Top 40 cassettes on the seat beside him, his Walkman headphones over, always, his ears. Frederick had made a name for himself even before his arrival at Grover Cleveland via the advanced utilization of his pronounced kleptomania; that is, Frederick Ames was a semi-professional thief. He lived in a creepy Victorian too near the Dewey Thruway, his father a gravedigger for Forest Lawn Cemetery and his mother, nebbish, a shut-in with a penchant for strays.

Frederick's skin was almost diaphanous: he looked like a cave-thing, bleached or otherwise improperly pigmented, and in this way propagated the Gothic bleakness that seemed inherent to his bloodline. I adored him and he knew it and, slowly, let me become his friend. On weekends we traveled by bus to Buffalo's Downtown, robbing most frequently the strange and cluttered 'everything' shops that all urban centers seem to possess. We took cameras, silk pocket squares for men's suits, shoe polish, coffee mugs. Frederick often worked with his Walkman on, perhaps to make him look more casual, perhaps to keep some part of himself from analyzing what the other part was doing. My job was to talk, to distract: Frederick and I were cousins, arriving in Buffalo from Pennsylvania to stay with relatives who had forgotten to collect us from the bus depot. With strange men who smelled of booze or smoke or curry, I pored over neighborhood maps in the Yellow Pages while Frederick filled up his bag. I realize now that Frederick made the more involved looting excursions without me; he would come to school dressed, for a freshman, to the nines: new Jordans, gold jewelry, a full-length sateen Bills parka. For spending so many weekends together our small talk was minimal, and consisted chiefly of single sentences uttered by Frederick while we waited for the bus: *My dad killed a cat with a shovel last night*, or, *my mom thinks the moon is an eye*. Implied in such statements was that I would never see the inside of Frederick's home, and only once did he see the inside of mine, being invited, by my parents, over to dinner the winter of that freshman year, the five of us eating chicken, green beans and mashed potatoes in silence. Afterward, over chocolate pudding, Frederick had commented on how bright our house was. You like the blue, my mom had said. (She had recently painted the kitchen.) No, Frederick had said, I mean you guys turn on a lot of lights.

Our sophomore year Fredrick began to steal cars. Sometime over summer his mother had been moved to a state-run facility, and with her departure went what little parenting Frederick received. Absent until lunch, Frederick would drive by the front of Grover Cleveland in a pilfered Skylark or Impala, his wan face glum. On the last balmy night of October, Frederick showed up at my house past one in the morning, waking me with bottle caps thrown at my second-story window. Frederick was drunk, and had a Porsche. I eased down the trellis in silence. We drove around some in the warm night air; the car's leather smelled new, and even at twenty-five miles an hour, it was clear what the Porsche's engine was capable of. At my feet was a half-finished six-pack of Labatt's Blue. Where'd you get the car, I asked. This world's spent meat, Frederick said back. We sped up, taking the neighborhood's turns more sharply, and I understood at that moment that I was okay, and Frederick was not. Three blocks from Grover Cleveland we passed a cop heading in the opposite direction, and shortly thereafter Frederick ceded what was left of his quickly eroding calm. He upshifted then lost control, the car hopping the curb and hitting a spruce ten yards from the high school's front doors. Stunned but conscious we sat in the smoking wreck, looking at each other. Frederick's head had connected with the steering wheel; one side of his face was already swelling, and above his eyebrows was wet, red blood. He looked like a survivor of a war fought a long time ago. Then Fredrick told me to run. The Porsche's shotgun door was bent in its frame, and I had to kick at it repeatedly to exit, sprinting down a side street and watching, peripherally, porch lights turn on, the homes' owners awoken by the impact. A mile later I stopped, out of breath and almost losing my night's dinner. I turned to see how far Frederick was behind me, but no one was there.

The next morning, at breakfast, all was explained: the superintendent had made the cursory round of phone calls to high-school faculty, and I came downstairs, freshly showered, to discover that Frederick had been apprehended at the scene, and was awaiting sentence while he lay, casted, on a gurney at Kaleida General. The cop we'd passed the night before had found Frederick behind the steering wheel, his leg broken, the Walkman's play button punched in. I never went to the hospital to visit him, believing such a trip would incriminate me. Frederick was sent to a detention center north of Syracuse; he did not return to Grover Cleveland and my heart, a coward's heart, was thankful. That night my father took us all out for dinner – a rare occurrence, the significance of which was not lost on me. On the trip home he strayed from the standard route, driving by the scene. The Porsche was still there. Buffalo is a poor city and damage control occurs slowly; the car had been unstuck from the tree, but a wrecker had yet to tow it to impound. It's awful what happened there, my dad said. It sure is, I answered. Are all families' secret thoughts Venn diagrams? Things that overlap and do not? That night I snuck back down the trellis. In my jeans pocket were two screwdrivers, borrowed from my father's garage workbench. Frederick, if you're out there, I have the Porsche's license plates. Convo me and I'll take down this listing. These items belong to you.

Starting Bid: $20.00

Antique Mahogany Chess Set. Pieces Hand-Carved (Bone). Late 19th Century. Traveling Set: Doors are Double-Hinged (Brass), Opening Up and then Out. Game Board is Inlaid – Alternating Mahogany and Rosewood. Dimensions: Box Closed: 11"x 6"x 3 ½"; Box Open (Including Doors): 20"x 12"x 2". All Pieces Intact. Light Scuffing/Burn Marks/Bloodstains along Bottom Left Corner. Made in Sri Lanka (Ceylon).

My brother Chase evolved to wunderkind the summer between my sophomore and junior years. Held back in kindergarten by his perceived inability to speak, he took the

SATs after middle school and scored in the top percentile. This result was enough for him to leapfrog three full grades, making Chase, at fourteen, a high-school senior. I was prepared to spend my days defending him physically but he was never once mistreated, Grover Cleveland's Class of '93 making him a sort of ad hoc mascot for intellectual endeavor. NYU felt the same way, and spring of that year my brother received a $15K renewable fellowship, along with tuition remission, and five months later moved from New York's second-largest city to its first. While uncoordinated to the point of klutzdom, Chase looked the most athletic in our small clan. He had a hockey player's build: broad shoulders with a narrow waist and chicken legs, his body thinning as one's eye moved down. We had the same hair, stick straight, a shade my mom's dad referred to as 'Irish Brown'. This same man would bestow upon my brother the aforementioned chess set, acquired by my great-grandfather during his years in the Merchant Marine. While not nautically inclined, I will admit a penchant, albeit romanticized, for traveling the seas via steam liner or some other outdated vessel, the world still enormous, wonder a possible thing.

For my family, these months were the happiest of any I can recall. My father, normally martinetish, loosened his proverbial neckwear: there was a trip to a water park, tickets to Bisons games. From the cheap seats of Dunn Tire we cheered and swatted bugs in the hot, white air. Summer ended, and we stuffed the minivan full of boxes and moved my brother to Brittany Residence Hall on East 10th Street, some five minutes from Manhattan's Washington Square. I recall no concern over whether or not it was truly a good idea for a fifteen-year-old to be living semi-independently in Greenwich Village, any dissent drowned out by the purple and white brochures that were arriving weekly to our Buffalo address. While our parents searched for hot sandwiches in the surrounding blocks, I sat with my brother on his vinyl dorm mattress. What do you think about all this, I asked. I don't think I thought about it at all, Chase said. The chess set was beside the bed, on his desk. Do you want to play, my brother asked. I'm not very good, I admitted. The face my brother made next was one of supreme fatigue: he brought his chin down, closing his eyes. His brow furrowed. At fifteen, the skin above my brother's eyes was creased. Okay, Chase said, but will you?

I think we fell victim to the ease of familiarity, a malady I imagine common to siblings who consider one another the closest of friends. I played chess with Chase that day and lost badly and, after a night at a nearby hotel with my parents, returned the next day to the other end of the state. Chase's roommate was from Taiwan, friendly but far from the things that he knew, and his homesickness kept him near-mute. I suppose the university (an institution my father would later try to sue) considered the best thing to do was pair Chase with someone wholly non-threatening, a social leper of sorts, who would not introduce my brother to the typical vices sought by those in their late teens. To say this plan backfired does not, perhaps, go far enough. Fall semester passed without incident, but Chase returned home for the winter break half terrified outsider and half angst-ridden quasi-adult. He'd undergone a latent growth spurt as well, adding another two inches to a frame that was having attention paid to it in NYU's weight room. Dinners were stern affairs, the thick silence broken only by my brother's obscenity-laced reviews of the food, the house, Buffalo itself. There was brief normalcy for December's last week, but with the Christmas trappings quickly outdated, the gloom, like a moat, encircled my brother once more. Chase left in January; I drove him to the Greyhound, my brother turning down my dad's offer of transport cross-state. In the gray light of the freezing depot, I hugged Chase goodbye. Visit, he told me, then boarded the bus. I did not. Two months later came a typed notice on school stationery: course work was strong but often missing, attendance patchy at best. Sometime in late March we lost contact, our calls answered only and always by the Taiwanese roommate, who informed us finally, and in mediocre English, *Chase take the chess set. He gone.*

Maw. A month of trips to Manhattan, our father taking leave from Grover Cleveland, a substitute in his stead. There were meetings with Provosts, waits at police stations.

There was a trip to the morgue, the John Does slid from their metal tombs, white sheets pulled down to show blue, still faces. Also: the minivan's ashtray, packed with cigarette butts; street performers in Washington Square, on stilts. My parents' meager savings, garnished by a second mortgage, went to the hiring of first one and then two private detectives who scoured the boroughs, Hoboken, points north. NYU put my parents up, when it could, in housing used for visiting faculty: there were long hours in leather armchairs, down pillows that did little to drown out the street noise below. I went with them some weekends but was still in school myself; I did no homework, sat stunned at my desk, and received straight As. College admissions notices arrived in the mail; I was a good student but a poor tester, with little interest in the extracurricular. Two SUNYs made offers but NYU turned me down, the thin envelope a dark cloud portending storm. My parents spoke little and grew gaunt. For a full week freezing rain slicked the roads, the world crystalline. And then news: a sighting in Newark, a grainy snapshot of someone in rags. It barely mattered if it was my brother or not: here was hope's wellspring, the long nightmare's end. We canvassed as though running for office, The Brick City's telephone poles clothed in our Xeroxed flyers. Door after door was answered, it seemed, by the same enormous black woman, her meaty arms spread for consolatory embrace as we gave thanks then descended the thirtieth, the fortieth, the eightieth porch. A third mortgage, the bank said, was out of the question. Winter turned to spring.

Chess, of course, often ends with no winner: there is the draw, the resignation, the fifty-move rule. My parents didn't give up so much as cede to logic: there were no tactics left to employ. They came back to Buffalo; I graduated in May; Chase jumped from the roof of a building in June. He'd been holding the chessboard when he went airborne, landing head first. Toxicology found traces of phencyclidine. Chase's last meal was bread. In a mortuary not far from Symphony Circle, I asked the funeral director how they'd put my brother's face back together. My mother was in an adjoining room, perusing caskets. Light baroque played from speakers in the walls. Well, the man said, looking to my father for intervention but finding none, in cases like your brother's, we insert a plate. He shifted from one foot to the other and I smiled; discomfort meant life, and it was a joyful thing to see. And this plate, I said, how will it look like my brother's face? Well, incisions are made at the temples, and here, the man said, pointing under the chin. So you peel back my brother's face and put the plate in, I said. That's right, the man said, as though he'd solved something. And what about the stuff that's in the way, I asked, the bone and such. My father was reading an unfolded brochure about flower arrangements, engrossed. The bone is sanded down or removed, the man said, his consternation growing. And how about his eyes, I asked. The eyes are untouched, the man said. And how about his soul, I said. Okay, my dad said. Okay, that's enough.

I put in two years at SUNY-Albany, fucked on drugs and not part of the world but not ever, really, wanting to die – as I mentioned already I have the heart of a coward, an organ so puny and useless it can subsist on next to nothing at all. I walked the campus at night in a long wool coat, drunk on gin and setting small fires in the bathroom sinks of empty school buildings. I trailed coeds until they jogged from fear. Tossed out, I packed up and struck west, sending a postcard to my parents bought at a gift shop in Dayton. A Unique Possession from a Bygone Era. Board's Hinges May Need Oil.

Starting Bid: $99.99

13" Tulipwood and Teflon Stiletto. Italian-Made (SKM). Single-Action OTF; Blade Retracts Manually. Length of Closed Knife is 7". Used Once.

Bad times in Decatur. The Midway Inn let you pay by the week, and I developed a dangerous friendship with the night clerk, a trailer-bred gun nut twice my age who sometimes kept minutes for the local chapter of a hate group called Lone Wolf. I was drunk always, beyond grace, and Wynn

Jost saw in me a lamb, someone whose psyche held all the worth of a torn kite, and was thereby open to suggestion via the newfound fraternity and acceptance provided by himself and other members of his ethnocentric cell. I worked at a meatpacking plant; I literally packed meat, wrapping T-bones in wax paper and boxing them, sixty-five per. The drone of industrial machinery was womblike, the white conveyor belt splotched, in patches, to pink. Some of Lone Wolf's goons worked here as well; a hulk named Jack Milk handed me, weekly, half-full cartons of cigarettes, the paper container's free space filled with hate literature meant to be distributed in the dark hours of predawn to mailboxes within walking distance of my motel. In this man's stone basement I sat on a metal folding chair, surrounded by a dozen of Central Time's Aryan zealots. The aforementioned Mr Jost, intellectual ringleader of this poor circus, forced these men (most of whom had not finished high school) to give reports on Nazi memorabilia Jost had purchased at trade shows in the Greater Illinois area. Trip-ups in reading words off the page were covered up by loud cries of White Power. An urn for coffee sat on a table under a German flag.

I was scared and lost and Jost was letting me live in the Midway for free, the owners absentee and unaware. I bought the switchblade at a pawnshop for protection, and three nights later Jost found it stashed beneath my mattress, tossing my room while I was out delivering pamphlets that explained why anyone not a Caucasian Protestant would lead the human race to Apocalypse. I should emphasize here, for clarity, that I really was starting to digest what was being fed to me: trauma (my brother) both debts and affords, the results often scary. Jost, along with Milk and three others, were waiting for me in my room when I returned that night. They drove me in Milk's Buick to an all-night gas station, where we waited for the next person of color to pull in. Forty minutes passed, the six of us crammed inside, listening to hate metal on low volume. Near dawn, an elderly black man shut off his Chrysler and entered the Conoco. He beelined for the bathroom; Jost handed me the knife. White Power, he said. White Power, I said, and got out.

What happened next was a miracle, so unearned I am sure that I cannot pay for it, ever, in this life. The black man stood at the sink, rinsing. He turned his head when he saw me come in. White Power, I said. What Power, he asked. I pulled the knife and sprung the blade. I saw all of you in that car, the man said. He had on a navy-blue baseball cap, the name of a naval destroyer spelled out in gold. So, I told him. The man unbuttoned then rolled up one sleeve of his dress shirt. Cut me, he told me. Here, on the arm. You're joking, I said. Do it, the man said. They won't come check on you. Do it. Right now. He moved his arm, bent at the elbow, out toward me. He wore glasses and had pleated khakis on. Come on, man, come on, you don't have the time.

He bobbed his arm up and down, his bare arm. I strode over to him and sliced. The blade sunk under the skin. The sound that he made was near to a yawn, a morning sound, a first sound of the day, then the man stumbled backward into the hand dryer. I dropped the knife and picked it up and turned and ran out of the store.

Back in the Buick I threw up on myself, the men of Lone Wolf cooing like bemused middle-schoolers, which I suppose in some ways they were. My accommodations gratis, I had a small nest egg stored, and once Jost's pickup departed from the Midway's lot that morning, I ran, at full speed, to the bus depot, buying a ticket for the next coach out. I wrapped the switchblade in my work shirt and mailed the bundle back home to Buffalo. Maybe you don't believe the story I've just told. I can only reply: lucky you.

Buy It Now: $10, Firm

Brown Mesh Trucker's Hat, 'Custer Gas Service, Custer, South Dakota' Printed on Front of Hat. Good Condition. Bill Rounded (Broken In). Ready to Wear.

A long engagement to one Katherine Anne Svenlund consumed over three years of my late twenties. Sioux Falls is a pleasant place and were I a different person, more even or stalwart, I might have managed an existence in that large village, continuing my work as night manager of Country Buffet #3847 and spending much of my free time browsing the ample selection of goods offered at the Salvation Army out near the airport. The Svenlund family is of fine Nordic stock, if genealogically naive, as their ancestors arrived to this country via propagandistic literature, specifically brochures and/or pamphlets that outlined the unequivocal agricultural promise of the Great Plains. (I should mention here, out of fairness, that these false promises were not limited to peoples of Norwegian descent nor just the acres comprising South Dakota; rather, America's new Robber Barons hired a great number of men to promote falsely that most of Middle America was a Farmers' Utopia – that places of near-apocalyptical aridity and barrenness were ripe wombs of earth, an agrarian delight, and that much of the middle part of the country was populated via the exacting of high levels of bullshit.)

Lone Wolf sent no minions to find me and I settled in, saving enough to afford a one-bedroom above a paint shop near the train tracks. I worked six days a week, sometimes seven, the staff at Country Buffet my surrogate family. One of my foster siblings was a short kind punk rocker named Tyler Banks. Tyler was five-five and washed dishes and sported a mohawk that changed colors with each new paycheck. He was always smiling and did no drugs and brought with him, to work, a small battery-powered boombox, which he set on a shelf above the sink, The Germs or Anti-Flag slamming it out while Tyler sprayed dishes clean. Night-times in Sioux Falls were slow affairs, our clientele mainly truckers and conspiracy theorists, the two demographics often overlapping. I'd started out bussing tables days but the turnover was constant, and within months had worked my way up to night manager. Through Tyler I'd made a small group of close friends, punkers and book nuts and anti-establishment crocheters, all of good heart and sound mind.

In autumn of '97, while I spoke with a trench-coated man about the '69 Apollo moon landing hoax, Katherine Anne Svenlund walked into Country Buffet. To say the restaurant's teal-carpeted environs were in direct contrast to her glamour would not do Katherine justice. Beneath my nametag, my heart leapt. She was five-ten and wearing tight indigo Levis. Red heels held thin, perfect feet. From a side pocket of her black leather biker's jacket Katherine removed a silver cigarette case. Her lipstick matched the shade of her footwear exactly. But beneath her vamp allure were the good values instilled upon her in youth; when she smiled, it was a smile of church Sundays and ribbons received at 4H events. It was a smile of wheat. Is Tyler here, Katherine asked. I'll get him, I said, but everything that was going to happen just had.

She moved in with me, the two of us watching Fellini movies and reading Dickinson aloud. Katherine ran the phones and did filing for a tow place; we lived modestly but never went without. Her parents, Meade County residents, generally approved of me; they worked cattle west of the river and had a small cabin in the Black Hills to which Katherine and I sometimes escaped, the mountain air at the west end of the state like no other air I have smelled. I saved in secret, telling no one other than Tyler of my plans. A year later, I walked into a downtown jeweler's and purchased a gold band with inlaid Idaho opal. When I took a knee and showed the ring to Katherine, her big eyes leaked: we would wed.

Setbacks – Mr Svenlund sustained a broken hip from being kicked by a heifer during calving; asbestos temporarily shut down the Country Buffet. We pushed the date back a year; I'd had meager communication with my parents, though they did know my whereabouts, and a month before the makeup date for the wedding a call came from my father: it was time to come home. Cancer had eroded my mother's lungs; the chemo worked and then didn't. I flew on an airplane for the very first time. The hospice aide was a Catholic ghost, so pious she seemed to float down the ward's halls. She spoke in soft tones, aroused by the misery of her workplace. The lobby's vending machines became close friends; I can still recall that C4 held Twix bars, H8 Junior Mints. My mom was tubes and skin on a gurney. I told her of Katherine; I told her I was sorry. Also: cold hands held with no words said; crows on telephones poles. Collapse.

After purchasing a second lot at Forest Lawn Cemetery, after the insurance money had come in, after my dad took early retirement from Grover Cleveland and sold off my childhood home, I packed up my duffel on my last night in town. At an all-night donut shop, my father wept over coffee. What do you want me to do, I said. Better, he told me, putting his Merit out on his bear claw. I flew back to Dakota but the bottom had dropped out of things there: Tyler had moved to LA to act in commercials, and ownership at the Country Buffet had switched hands. Katherine, too, had vanished, disappearing into Proust's seven volumes just as autumn set in. The choice to terminate the union was as democratic and affable as such a decision can be, but I still wonder what my life might have been like had things gone differently: the Midwest is this country's best wonder, and to know again the pastoral life, where small things mattered, where big clouds moved like ships across wide blue skies, the fields windswept, the post-and-wire clocklike, its taut lengths measuring the course of each day – to return again ever would bring about a sort of devastating grace I'm not prepared for. Talcum Applied to Hat's Interior Lining, to Get Out the Smell.

Starting Bid: $3.99

Mason Jar of Eighteen Rattlesnake Tails. Vacuum-Sealed. Glass is Aqua, Reads 'Mason's Patent, October 31st, 1864'. Tails Guaranteed Authentic; Still Rattle.

For me, our country's true west is not its coast but rather that odd strip that comprises the western part of Mountain Time, and the eastern part of Pacific – here are your Renos, your Provos, your Yumas, Pocatello and St George and Butte. Here the word 'hardscrabble' seems not sentimental but correct, the mesa erasing everything, the Rockies and Tetons stern reminders that humans are but minor canker, a virus that with time will be flushed out. I spent six months in Elko, Nevada, working third shift at a gas station tucked to one side of I-80. My rented doublewide stood just across the interstate, and each dawn I crossed the blacktop on foot, this trek emblematic of the fact that I was not living the life that most people were, that here one had a road that ran from Oakland all the way to New York, that millions each year crossed east to west or west to east and I, without car or bank account, without obligation to spouse, child or family, without mortgage or any other mile marker common to status-quo American existence, could get across in under thirty seconds, and be home.

My co-worker was a middle-aged Chicana named Aura. Her daughter, jailed for possession with intent, had left her in charge of two grandsons, who slept on the white beveled linoleum behind the register, under twin fleece Wal-Mart Cookie Monster blankets. My first month I bought a computer from a 'traveling salesman', a Mormon-turned-methhead who had stolen an automobile in Boise and was willing to sell me the Compaq desktop unit for one-quarter of the going price. I bought in, an installer coming to my trailer the next day. Here was the world, shrunk to pixels. I couldn't figure out why anyone cared. I unplugged the device, spending those winter days watching snow bloat the desert. But vice thrives on intrigue and with time I plugged back in, locating individuals (see below post) who viewed this new medium in a manner not dissimilar to how Thoreau viewed the railroads: that what was being built was also taking away, that the tech boom was not trend but monster, a dark thing with sharp edges that preyed upon the more craven tendencies of human society, and sought to destroy connection through mimicry of connection, private industry now making the rules for the very ways in which we, as a species, would interact. Or something like that. For a while the banter was static catharsis, fun if a little bit odd, but with time the irony of such persiflages produced in me deep melancholy: we had to pay in to the very thing we sought to critique. Spring came and I set the device by the highway. A day later, it was gone.

Aura's grandsons, Rodolfo and Rogelio, presented me with the snake tails on my last night of work. The gas station mandated that two employees always be present, the ideology being that this coupling would somehow stave off felonious acts. And they may have been right: my half-year in Elko passed without incident. But it was too much seeing those children sleep under cheap and highly flammable blankets night after night, and I often told Aura to come late or leave early, doctoring her time card myself. The boys fought as they handed over my gift, each wanting to be the chief presenter. And where did you get these, I asked, bending down. Out there, said Rodolfo, pointing past the pumps, the jar almost dropping. I took a bus out of town, skimming California's coastline before settling, homeless, in Santa Cruz, the cool sand under the boardwalk's planks home to a coven of vagabonds from all ends of the Earth.

To this day I have no idea how Aura and her grandsons ultimately came to possess one and a half dozen tails of venomous reptiles, but I have, as stated in the item description, verified the tails' authenticity, taking the jar to a taxidermist in the Bronx, who in turn referred me to a herpetologist at Rutgers-New Brunswick. Tails are divided between two varieties: Great Basin (*Crotalus viridis lutosus*) and Panamint (*Crotalus mitchellii stephensi*). While neither species is considered particularly antagonistic, if cornered they both will stand their ground.

Starting Bid: $16.99

Black Low-Top Chuck Taylors (Pre-Nike Era!!!). Heavily Used. Hole in Rubber Sole of Right Shoe approx. 3/5 inch in Diameter. (Hole Has Been Filled With Wad of Paper Napkins Taken From A Churros Stand at the Santa Cruz

Beach Boardwalk). Color Faded. One (1) Eyelet Missing Metal Ring. Size 11½.

Denouncing all manner of helotry, I bought a bus ticket from Santa Cruz to Seattle, arriving the week before the WTO conference and locating, amidst the impending rioters, a half-dozen online acquaintances, not quite socialists but something closer, perhaps, to secular nihilists – rich kids, products of divorce, MENSA types with chips on their shoulders, who by their mid-twenties had been bailed out of jails all over the country by lawyers retained by their parents; kids who had grown up on the Upper West Side and gone on to Choate or St Paul's or Andover, and afterward formed a small tribe of like-minded individuals hell-bent on vandalism (facts I had learned through repeated excursions to the Santa Cruz Public Library, a place sympathetic to ideologies like mine, an institution that has resisted wholly the sensational hegemony of the Patriot Act – that would rather read Orwell than live it – a place that fully endorsed the idea of someone who had been sleeping on the beach for a week, unshowered, sitting down and using a computer to exchange messages with a group planning violence, as long as the violence spoke out against larger violence, which the violence in Seattle really meant to) – and with the vapors of tear gas roiling about us, providing a berserk sort of vestment, this small crew and I removed a public trash can from its foundation, rocked and then ripped the can free from where it was bolted to the concrete, and while I cannot take credit for actually launching the can through the plate-glass storefront of NikeTown, I most certainly did enter the spacious, high-ceilinged shop and wrecked everything I could before an agent of law forcibly detained me for theft, which is to say these very shoes, made by a company subsequently bought out by Nike, destroyed a multitude of shelves, boxes, clothing racks and other props inside the store. As I had no rich parents to bail me out of jail, I watched my beleaguered cohorts exit the King County holding cell we had shared for the past seventy-two hours, each vowing that they would make sure that their legal representation found a way to afford me a similar freedom. These promises turned out to be empty, and I was held for nearly a month before my day in court, where a female judge wore the same terse frown for a full twenty minutes before assigning me a very heavy fine, which I haven't paid a cent of.

Starting Bid: $8.99

Lot of Mets Paraphernalia, Years 2003-08. Ten Pennants, Three T-Shirts, Two 'Bobbleheads' (Piazza and Martinez). Keychain. Inflatable Bat.

And there were more travels, too, trips worn like coats, heavy journeys, all by bus; things that now seem at once fictive and real, not lived but experienced, as I stalled and balked, trying hard never to commit, never to settle. In Denton, Texas, I was involved in a fist fight on Fry Street. In Tulsa, I had an affair with a topless dancer, her husband a tornado chaser and retired seismologist. We were discovered after an F4 didn't pan out, the man walking in while we kissed in the kitchen and subsequently screaming that I was doom's chattel, the paw of Satan himself. There were months spent in Mobile, Atlanta and Miami. There was my year in Cleveland, running bags at a fancy hotel. But with time these jumps summed to nothing, and, tired and empty, I finally went home. My father, with whom I had been in touch intermittently, had moved to Long Island City, his pension and part-time math tutoring just enough. I arrived on his doorstep, windblown. Time had taken: my father's hair had turned white. We sat in twin recliners in his small living room. I'm ready to stick around now, I told him. I've dreamed that, that you said that, my father said back.

The New York Transit Authority is always looking for a few good men, and I got a job as a Customer Service Rep at Grand Central. I'm still here, sitting while so many move. My father and I have season bleacher seats at Citi, the Metties breaking our hearts every year. The ramp to Grand Central's lower concourse possesses improbable acoustical properties, and in those rare moments when things are slow, a single person will descend its length and pass under the archway, the sound of their footfalls dancing up to the ceiling, and it's all I can do to keep myself seated, to not rise from my faux-leather desk chair and scream at them take me with you, I will pay any amount. Is there a trick to this life that I'm missing? Some clue, unfound? At the ballpark are beef franks, soft pretzels, hot mustard. My commute in from Queens is easy, off-hours. But I can't quite convince myself to buy in completely, and my dad now has a fake hip from a fall, and the bills are like virus, dormant then outbreak, and I can't house this stuff because I can't keep it near me, can't see it each day and know more stuff is out there, while I wait here, an anchor, the son now returned, as epics are written and statues constructed and buses, at night-time, rush along highways, always going somewhere better, somewhere else.

Starting Bid: $9.99

Original Copy of Toast from the Banks-Skyzwack Wedding Reception, Orange County Country Club, July 16th, 2006. Paper is Slightly Yellowed (Time) and has Large Merlot Stain in Right Bottom Corner. Legibility of Text Remains Unaffected.

I should state here that it wasn't just me that was against the Banks-Skyzwack union, but rather that the group of friends I had known from my time in the Midwest found this merger so unsavory that many of them actually boycotted the event, and that in accepting my role of best man there were two starkly different demographics pressuring me with their agendas, the first being the friends I just mentioned, the second being the bride and groom. While I did and do admit to a predilection for spirits, Tyler and his fiancée's selfishly exaggerated concern in regard to my imbibing ultimately translated to me being forced to sleep at the foot of Kyla Skyzwack's childhood bed, the bride and groom inches away, snoring in tandem on Kyla's spring-coiled Serta twin so as to make sure I remained sober the night before their big day. But let me back up: Tyler Banks, once punk-rock dishwasher, was now a porn mogul, having landed in Chatsworth at just the right time to be a part of smut's jump into cyberspace.

Tyler found me through my place of employment, my name listed on some page of the MTA's website. I tell myself I flew west out of loyalty, though I know it has much more to do with a dysfunctional lusting after things long passed. Arriving at John Wayne, I found Tyler and his bride-to-be in baggage claim, tanned and dead inside. The subsequent days only brought proof of this, the wedding party dining at a Cheesecake Factory in Brentwood, where Kyla, an employee of Tyler's Tens (in addition to a multitude of other pay sites), flashed her enormous fake breasts to a group of Japanese tourists, who in turn held up their end of this tasteless cliché by taking copious amounts of pictures with their digital cameras. Tyler's own parents sat smiling, Midwestern and horrified. Both of Kyla's parents were Hollywood lawyers and devoid of moral pretense, caring less about what their daughter did than that the millions would keep coming, never mind the source. The last straw was the procurement, by Tyler, of an entourage of mid-tier adult stars, from which I could pick as many or as few as I wanted to have my way with. This wretched attempt at a gift occurred in a private room of a West Hollywood nightclub, Tyler producing a key to a suite at a nearby hotel. I chose a single female, had the taxi drop her off a block away, and went to the room alone, where I wrote the below speech in full:

A toast then, while we can, while youth graces us, while our faces shine, while our hair is coiffed in a manner that inspires true envy, while our fingernails possess no chips, nothing hanging, while our organs are determined and hearty, while our good teeth remain intact in their gums, need not root canals, need not extraction, need not to be worked on while we sit in a chair that has been reclined mechanically, trying to think of something better to think about, the birds lighting past the window, the dental saw whirring; while we wake without tingling in one of our limbs, before our blouses and cap toes and cuts of our jeans plunge inevitably toward obsolescence, prior to the consideration of vitamin supplements, prior to repeat excursions to outlet wholesalers because the thatched Javan magazine rack is backordered; while there's a tap in our toes, a cut to our jib, while vibrancy still speckles the iris, while beds go unmade and floors function as hampers and we know all the songs on the radio, and our skin is not squamous from the aging of cells and we do not lurch down the hallways of rest homes, before ducks in neat rows and the long gloam of August, before the cold front, the squall line, the wind shift, a lifting of glasses, a jubilant hoisting, because we have made it this far mainly intact, because no act has crushed us to palsied, because it's 6:32 on a June night in Tustin and the back room of this hall is ours for the full of the evening, a time during which we will not be hurtled toward loss, toward our own peculiar miseries, will sit here with wine and not age and not die for we possess immortal capacity, something better than hope, because hope is for the weak, is for the needy, is for middle-aged dads six months past divorce, is for the octogenarian who prays before bedtime that her SSI checks will outlast her – these people need hope, that gold, hollow thing, and we, while here, while dining, need nothing – need only for our drinks to be freshened up, need only to have the food keep coming.

* * *

Because we had been promised that the food *would* keep coming, were assured by a bevy of antediluvians (whom we did or did not cast our votes for) that the shelves would be full, that the taps would run clean, that there would be *unending smorgasbord*, as this country, while we were still glints in the eye, still tears in the condom, had chosen McDonald's, not McGovern, had fueled, oiled and lubed the corporate machine, *had cared more about product than service*, and so then new odes: to the plasma TV, to the next batch of modified food additives, to pay sites devoted to horny young teens; to bugs in the code and data corruption; to Diebold's firm grasp on Ohio, to the image, long passed, of Saddam in beret, grasping the hilt of a saber, gauging the weight of the gold-handled sword per a series of terse chopping motions – Saddam is testing a weapon – to a long list of lies that we'll be left to explain to our children and then to our grandchildren, should we not die on the roads, in the air, from disease – to tunnel vision, because as long as we can keep both eyes on the road, we do not need to look at the landscape, and as long as there's gas and asphalt and rubber trees, we can keep driving without *destination*, a word we know not what to do with, a word and idea, we're really pretty sure, that somebody else was supposed to take care of, while we leased SUVs and ate maki rolls and attained thorough knowledge of Wall Street's big gainers, and since we know nothing, since the directions were lost, since all manner of order was tossed out the window, as we enter this century grasping at straws and pointing with fingers, I urge, while you can, listen less and see more, before what lies ahead turns to dots in the rear-view, before life is a marker long passed and well gone – steal these candlesticks, fill your coat up with forks, and hurry along into the night; do not let this world catch up with you, ever, and if it knocks, do not let it in.

The speech was read once in its entirety. A second reading was halted by the disc jockey, a for-hire guy by the name of Lenny Tarveck who, as it turns out, was also from Buffalo, and grew up not all that far from me.

Starting Bid: $1

MANY GRACIOUS THANKS

Thanks to my family, without whom not one word of what I write would be possible. Thanks to all at Harvill Secker/Vintage for their belief in and care with this collection, and especial thanks to Frances Jessop and Stuart Williams. Thanks to all my friends: DDS, PHS Peeps, SG Peeps, IC Peeps. Many thanks to the UVA MFA Program and the Fine Arts Work Center, and all of the amazing people I met at those places. Many thanks to Martha Heasley Cox and the Center for Steinbeck Studies. Many thanks to my teachers and many thanks to my students. Many gracious thanks to the editors of the magazines and anthologies in which these stories first appeared. And you – thank *you*.